REVIEWER'S COMMENTS FOR
ON THE COUNT

On The Count is an often poignant, often funny, often tragic, and often upsetting look at life behind bars. It is always true and real about what life, living conditions, working conditions, and the constant stressors of being behind bars is really like. Mike has succinctly captured life "on the yard" from both an inmate's perspective, and more importantly, a staff perspective. In the last decade or so, there have been some books published from an inmate's perspective of life behind bars. There have been none that have so accurately captured life for a staff member behind bars. Unlike inmates, the staff are behind the bars voluntarily, in some cases for a longer period of time than the inmates they are serving. The stories Mike tells and experiences he shares come from someone who has a long and close working relationship with inmates and staff. His experiences will leave you laughing, crying, fearful and hopeful, but above all, will leave you amazed at what really goes on in a maximum security prison. For anyone who is interested in working in such a facility (or who now does), this is a must read. For anyone else who simply wants to glimpse what goes on in daily life "on the yard," this is an authoritative source. This is one of those books that must be "ON YOUR SHELF!"

Dr. Wayman C. Mullins
Professor, Department of Criminal Justice
Texas State University

Jackie & Charley,
Hope you enjoy this book
about the first ten years of my
career as a psychologist.

ON THE COUNT
Madness, Humor, and
Mental-Health Care in a
Maximum-Security Prison

Best Wishes,
Mike Boccia

Michael B. Boccia, Ph.D

authorHOUSE®

AuthorHouse™
1663 Liberty Drive
Bloomington, IN 47403
www.authorhouse.com
Phone: 1-800-839-8640

First published by AuthorHouse   11/8/2011

ISBN: 978-1-4670-6026-4 (sc)
ISBN: 978-1-4670-6167-4 (hc)

Library of Congress Control Number: 2011919157

Printed in the United States of America

DISCLAIMER

Although based on actual people and events, the specifics of some of the events and locations depicted in this book and the names of the characters involved have been changed to protect their identity and save them from any embarrassment.

CONTENTS

PREFACE

On The Count is a fictionalized narrative of actual events that took place over a ten-year span in the early professional experiences of a forensic psychologist we will call Dr. Martin Barilla. From 1971 to 1974, Dr. Barilla worked in mental-health services at Henry Ford Hospital for less than one year, and then he worked for nearly three years at the criminal court, called Recorders Court, and county-jail system. Both of these professional experiences were in Detroit, Michigan. Then, Dr. Barilla moved back to Massachusetts to work for several years in a hospital for the criminally insane, Martinsville State Hospital, followed by his work in a maximum security prison, Centerville Correctional Facility, from 1977 to 1981.

On The Count is an anecdotal, tutorial, ten-year narrative that exposes the reader to everyday realities in a maximum-security prison and other security treatment settings, namely a county jail clinic and a hospital for the criminally insane. The decade from 1971 to 1981 was an exciting and challenging period in correctional settings, especially the fictionally named but real Centerville Correctional Facility. Dr, Barilla's story, including descriptions of events, inmates, and correctional staff, is told primarily by narrating his pointed tutorial conversations with the people living together within forty-five acres behind the tower-guarded, thirty-foot perimeter walls.

The book presents a combined message of realism, hope, danger, humor, perseverance, and the potential rewards for the formidable, sometimes successful, work of correctional care.

This retrospective journey with Dr. Barilla may change the way the reader thinks about maximum-security prison, rehabilitation, and punishment. The reader will learn about numerous applications of psychological principles in managing inmates and treating inmate-patients in the dangerous prison environment. Hopefully, the book will inspire some readers to consider pursuing a career in correctional care and also strengthen the resolve and skill of those dedicated people already in the corrections profession.

The title, *On The Count*, was a term Dr. Barilla found used in correctional facilities that meant a physical count was about to be made of all inmates in order to insure that every prisoner was accounted for. This count might come every morning or every night when the inmates were secured in their cells or after each meal. Anytime during the day or night, a physical count can be called for on the spot. At the announcement, "On the count," each inmate needed to be in his cell.

Contrary to this, the term "off the count" meant that an inmate was missing, had escaped, or may have been murdered. In fact, to "off" someone was a common expression for committing murder.

The responsibility for the safety, welfare, and count of inmates rested upon the corrections officer who was assigned to a particular unit, called a company or gallery, usually consisting of forty-two men. The design of all adult maximum-security prisons was for many years uniformly standardized so that there were three tiers of cells stacked one upon the other, with each tier housing forty-two inmates. These cells stood back to back with a similar set of cells, which likewise, rose three stories high. They were mirror images of each other.

There were also other terms that began with "on the..." and indicated to the inmates that a specific activity was presently to take place. For example, "on the yard" meant it was time to go outside for recreation, or "on the chow" meant it was time to go to the mess hall to eat. Inmates were called for "on the visit," when they had a visitor. "On the program" was a call for inmates to report to their vocational program (for example, knit shop, auto shop, carpenter shop) and to go to the specific location for that activity, escorted by a correctional officer, who were universally known as COs. One additional "on" command was for the occasion when a CO determined that there was too much noise generated by inmates, which could disrupt the smooth functioning of a particular company or cellblock, and the officer might angrily, or at least in a very assertive manner, yell out, "On the noise! On the noise!" And that command meant to stop all the crazy yelling, screaming, or whatever, and calm down and act civilized.

These were all commands and expressions used in the system to make inmates aware of something they were expected, sometimes mandated, to do. Sometimes going to the yard, for example, was voluntary, but usually the "on" commands meant the inmates had to comply with the command bellowed out by the CO who controlled their particular company or cellblock.

Six companies comprised one cellblock, which contained 250 inmates. Each cellblock was lettered (A,B,C,D, etc.), and groups of cellblocks were divided in most prisons into east and west, depending upon which direction they were facing. Some prisons, depending on their size, configuration, and population, may have had further unofficial designations, which indicated a specific group of cells for a certain group of trouble-making inmates, such as, "Nairobi," or "Watts."

Then, as explained by Dr. Barilla, there were other specific groups of inmates housed in certain units depending upon their needs, such as elderly, handicapped, mentally retarded, or protective-custody units. These were all still inmates, and they too, even with their individual needs and escorted by COs, were mandated to respond to the call, "on the count."

Although described above in past tense, the conditions and practices in most older prisons in the Northeast, including Centerville Correctional Facility, have continued unchanged for many decades beyond the time period of this story.

When I first arrived to go to work in what I'm calling the Centerville Correctional Facility, I remembered something I had done when I had worked for the criminal court in Detroit. I had called a psychologist in the massive Jackson Prison, which housed seven thousand inmates and indignantly challenged his efforts at rehabilitating inmates in his prison, while I also alluded to the high recidivism rate of released inmates. Now, I suddenly realized that *I* was the psychologist responsible for rehabilitating convicted and sentenced felons—in a maximum-security prison's mental hospital no less. I felt inadequate, anxious, and I questioned my competence to be a forensic psychologist, working with imprisoned, mentally ill felons in this overwhelming environment.

I had already, during my previous short tenure at Martinsville State Hospital for the criminally insane, been called "motherfucker" by numerous inmate-patients, and on at least two occasions, inmate-patients threatened to remove my genitalia! It was no secret that a considerable percentage of hospital personnel were, at any given time, out on compensation due to injury and assaults from the inmate-patients. It occurred to me that I could get hurt in this often-violent environment.

I had to quickly invent some "pro" reasons in my mental pros/cons ledger to persevere in this job instead of leaving *stat*, to borrow a nursing term. Also, I had trouble losing a cynical fantasy, borrowed from Dante's *Inferno*, of a big placard I imagined in the vestibule of Martinsville State Hospital: ABANDON ALL HOPE, YE WHO ENTER HERE!

Mike Boccia, Ph.D.

ACKNOWLEDGMENTS

Decades of gratitude are due to Donna Heath Boccia, who always encouraged and supported my many career pursuits and who assertively moved me and inspired me to tell this story.

Special thanks to Peter Mars, my co-author and mentor, who gave me confidence, direction, his literary expertise, and ignited my excitement in writing *On The Count.*

Appreciation to Sheri Roman, who helped me organize my thoughts and professional experiences in preparation for writing this story.

Many thanks to my mental health colleagues who taught me and supported me; my correctional colleagues who taught me and protected me; and my inmate-patients who taught me and took away something of value for their rehabilitation.

Amidst the violence, madness, and incredibly formidable challenges in maximum-security prisons, some quixotic notion was that this mental-health mission was possible.

Chapter 1

The Real Deal: A Brief Orientation about Maximum Security Prisons

Over the many years that he had been a clinical psychologist at the Martinsville Security Treatment Center, a hospital for the criminally insane, Dr. Barilla had been exposed to the minds of quite a number of people who had committed atrocities, which were the result of an unstable psyche and some kind of personality disorder. Having practiced both within the confines of a mental institution as well as in a private setting, it was as though there was not a person in the world, including himself, who could pass as a truly sane individual. It seemed to him that, to a degree, everyone suffered from some sort of mental or emotional problems. It also seemed difficult for the mental health profession to establish a universal profile for a so-called normal person.

After many years in the correctional mental health system, Dr. Barilla really enjoyed giving his psychology students at Concord College in Massachusetts, most of whom were in criminal-justice studies, a sound understanding of the culture of a maximum-security prison.

Invariably, students in the doctor's psychology classes wanted to digress from the lesson plan to pick Dr. Barilla's brain and hear about his experiences in prison. This curiosity was willingly tolerated by Adjunct Professor Barilla, and he developed an extensive explanation of the history of mental-health care in prison that he presented in the form of a mini-lecture:

1

"Had it not been for the integration between established mental-health practices and the penal system that resulted from a number of changes that were enacted by social activists and mental-health professionals back in the late 1970s and early 1980s, this benefit would never have come into play.

"The ultimate goal was to work with inmate-patients in an effort to help them to eventually obtain jobs and rejoin the general public.

"Likewise, at the same time, a decision was made to 'deinstitutionalize' and assimilate into halfway houses patients who had been locked away in the mental wards of civil hospitals. Many of these mentally-challenged patients were allowed to have a relatively normal lifestyle with better, more comfortable sleeping quarters, opportunities for shopping, day trips, visitations with families, work responsibilities within the dwelling with other half-way house patients, and, for most, an eventual opportunity for freedom to walk about neighborhoods and parks. Such patients' families embraced the idea.

"However, the corrections community, both inmates and prison employees, objected strongly to changing the status of those who had been *patients* housed in hospitals for the criminally insane to the designation as *inmate-patients* housed in a maximum-security prison. Those opposed to the changes feared an increase in the instability of the prison culture by mixing mentally ill inmates in an already violent environment."

Dr. Barilla recalled, "In my early years at Martinsville Security Treatment Hospital, I had lots of naïveté concerning my new appointment at the state facility. My first thought when I entered the world of prison mental healthcare was: *mission impossible?* I thought this because the first thing one must do is come to an understanding of what imprisonment means and what kind of psych treatment is possible in such an environment. Simply put, imprisonment can be described as a process of controlling and structuring convicted felons' lives with two goals that are desirable from the criminal-justice perspective: first, the segregation of prisoners from the free community, and secondly, rehabilitation, which for many includes mental health care."

Dr. Barilla continued, "While modern prisons are neither directed toward deterrence through punishment nor effectively rehabilitative in general, there seems to be some interaction of the two forces as described by British penologist, Ruggles-Brise, in 1912. He said, 'Our constant effort is to hold the balance between what is necessary as punishment from a penal and deterrent point of view, and what can be conceded, consistently with this, in the way of humanizing and reforming influences.'"

Dr. Barilla noted, "One must also remember that inmate-patients suffer from two distinct problems: the first being the traditional mental-illness disorders such as bipolar disorder, clinical depression, anxiety disorders, and schizophrenia—all called Axis I disorders. These disorders are usually believed by mental-health psychiatrists to be related to genetic predisposition and chemical imbalance, resulting in various emotional and mental challenges.

"The second problem is the personality disorder, which typically is associated with deficits in healthy character development. These are called Axis II disorders. Axis II disorders basically result from a long-term, negative developmental process, usually attributable to a primary caregiver's influence, self-defeating habit formation, and various negative environmental influences. The latter might include poor neighborhoods and the persons who reside in those subcultural communities who help the subjects develop these negative patterns (for example, emulation of those who are a negative influence in the community such as pimps and drug dealers).

"In a penitentiary, it is very common to have inmates suffer from Axis II disorders in which they display antisocial personalities and which are often shown in their sociopathic or psychopathic characteristics. Some common traits include individuals who have little or no conscience, do not profit from past experience or mistakes, and are very predatory, selfish, and impulsive. This is further explained by the fact that criminal types are strongly reinforced by the rewards that they experience—that is, by the fruits of their criminal behavior, such as the possessions they gain from stealing money and other valuables. To summarize, when the rewards for an individual like that far outweigh the negative consequences, the criminal behavior strengthens and persists.

"There also needs to be a greater understanding of these problems because what you have in prison is really kind of a pervasive dual diagnosis. This particular term, dual diagnosis, has often been used for people with drug addiction and mental illness (substance abuse coupled with an Axis I disorder), but I have also heard it used with some veracity to label people who have character disorders and some form of mental illness in the penitentiary. The great majority of people serving time in prison—being, of course, human beings who have experienced various kinds of problems in life with accompanying failures, relationships gone bad, or abandonment or rejection—often also experience some Axis I disorder in addition to some form of personality disorder.

"Add to that the fact that there are a lot of people with character disorders who have drug and alcohol addictions and mental illness—a burden of three disorders—with the most critical condition in terms of effective rehabilitation being the character disorder (Axis II), which tends to receive the least attention in treatment endeavors. Too often mental-health professionals only focus on the Axis I disorders and do not pay adequate treatment attention to the troublesome character and personality disorders. These Axis II disorders usually begin very early in life and, subsequently, are very difficult to change. In plain terms, for a person in prison who is depressed and has a personality disorder, it is very likely that the personality disorder existed long before he ever became depressed. The symptoms of depression might be alleviated with help by a mental-health professional. However, changing an antisocial personality back into a caring, pro-social person who will be happy to live by the Golden Rule, caring about other people, and never again thinking about committing crimes or harming people, would be extremely difficult."

Student Tony Siskel, asked, "Doc B, is *every* inmate or inmate-patient a person with a serious character disorder?"

Doctor Barilla nodded his head twice, indicating both "yes" and "no," and with a smile he suggested that this was an important question.

"There is a little piece of information that ought to be brought back to the discussion on Axis I and Axis II diagnoses—specifically, the diagnosis of antisocial personality disorder. Research has indicated pretty clearly that over 80 percent of inmates serving time—certainly those serving time in a maximum-security prison where inmates typically arrive with considerably lengthy records—could be diagnosed with the Axis II antisocial personality disorder. Why would that be important to know: This is important in reference to the traditional practice of mental health in correctional facilities where they are targeting only the kinds of problems of Axis I, such as depression, anxiety, and schizophrenia disorders. These are the disorders that are given the attention just as they are in civil psychiatric hospitals in the free community, and that is important. However, the problem is that many professionals believe Axis II disorders, which are longstanding, are not very treatable or certainly not easily treatable, especially antisocial personality disorders. These have been given very little attention and have not been treated successfully. This reality is validated by the very high recidivism rate found among most released prisoners in most states. Some estimates are anywhere from 68 to70 percent, all the way up to 85 percent!"

Student Jane Daggert, asked, "Could you please spell out the main traits in a person with antisocial personal disorder?"

"Gladly," Doctor Barilla answered. "Some of the important hallmarks, as previously mentioned, of antisocial personality behavior are poor conscience development, inability to learn from negative experiences, impulsiveness, predatory behavior, little or no remorse for wrongdoing, selfishness, and lack of empathy. In the extreme cases of sociopathy, the question becomes: are those involved in working with these types of inmates talking about rehabilitation or 'habilitation'? Many inmates have lived rather primitive lifestyles and never really have had meaning, direction, discipline, and sound education in pro-social behavior. The mission of the office of mental health in prison settings is to undertake a full range of mental-health care, based on a community mental-health model to stabilize inmate-patients, and to continue with follow-up care and treatment while inmate-patients remain in prison. Part of the mission of mental-health care is to assimilate inmate-patients, especially the seriously ill, into the general prison population to participate in all or part of the programs that are available to them and that will enable them to continue a meaningful lifestyle within the corrections community. The purpose of this assimilation is the ultimate preparation for the possible eventual reentry of inmate-patients into the free community, depending upon the severity of their prison sentence."

Tony Siskel asked another important question, "Doc B., how much help do you get from others to do this tough work?"

"Wow! Yeah—yeah!" came the response from some of those in the room.

Doctor Barilla pondered, then answered, "In order to achieve effective mental-health care, it is critical that the services are provided by a multidisciplinary mental-health team. No single doctor or nurse or therapist can do this job alone. The effective team also includes corrections staff, family, loved ones, clergy, and volunteers."

It was important for Dr. Barilla to help students understand that many inmates and inmate-patients are fixated at some emotional and behavioral level of adolescence.

He continued, "Many of these individuals have never really matured in terms of their socialization, emotional expression and development, and cognitive functioning, such that one might perceive correctional personnel as being, collectively, like surrogate parents. To paraphrase Alfred Adler, the famous Freudian disciple, individuals at this level of maturation misbehave for four different reasons: revenge, power, attention, and to show that they are emotionally disabled so that the 'disability' will almost guarantee that somebody will take care of them and give them attention.

"After mentioning the traits of character disorder, especially the lack of remorse, one might wonder about the current terminology of 'correctional facility,' as opposed to the former terminology 'penitentiary,' which was based on the root word 'penitence.' The change in word usage must have come about by the very fact that prison officials did not find too many penitent inmates who were convicted and sentenced to prison. And, then again, since there have been correctional facilities for decades, whatever happened to 'correction' in correctional facilities: it doesn't seem like enough positive change is going on in that area either."

Sally Griner, an impatient but dedicated student, blurted out, "Is there a lot of tension in prison around issues of appearing tough, defending one's self, etc.?"

Doctor Barilla replied, "That's true, but the situation is somewhat complex with inmates who become mentally ill and become inmate-patients. It is also important to understand that there's a very strong machismo culture in prison, especially at the level of maximum security. Incarcerated individuals frequently pump iron, strut around acting mean and tough, and spout mottos such as, 'Don't be kind because kindness is a sign of weakness.' Inmates in a maximum-security prison are usually multiple offenders, often having been in prison and county jail a number of times. Most have been on probation, sometimes many times, and most have been in juvenile hall as youngsters. The majority have had drug or alcohol problems. They usually have had longer sentences than those in lower security levels of incarceration, and often are acting-out individuals—bad actors— who do not function well in medium or minimum-security prisons."

Doctor Barilla moved on to issues that prison staff need to cope with in the tough environment of maximum-security.

"We discovered that usually it is healthy to remain unaffected by the display of the volatile temperament and actions of the inmates. Related to that, we found the value of utilizing mantras that are pretty repetitious and that follow most professionals throughout their career. One such example, when facing a difficult challenge, is to consistently tell yourself, 'Good jail, good jail!' in order to help acquire self assurance and to give off a kind of false bravado, because there are situations in jail and prison that are a bit scary and can be very dangerous. One cannot go around being fearful all the time or having a lot of anxiety about difficult challenges. If that happens, then one cannot work in a place like a maximum-security prison because the net effect is burnout and eventual loss of one's employment.

"Maximum-security prisons are usually larger than other facilities and have a fulltime psychiatric staff, and the best ones have the whole community, mental-health model with psychiatrists, psychiatric nurses, psychologists, social workers, recreational therapists, occupational therapists, and so on, along with the correctional officer contingent, and a lot of other resources. A few of these positions, especially psychiatric nurses, usually operate around the clock, seven days a week. The maximum-security prisons, in many states, typically cover forty to fifty acres inside a thirty-foot-high perimeter wall with twelve gun towers. Within these confines there are usually a number of vocational programs. Typically, those programs include a knit shop, an auto-body shop, a furniture or carpentry shop, and lots of educational programs as well, including GED and college courses."

Joe Collins, one of several COs in the psychology class, asked Doctor Barilla, "What's the biggest prison you've ever heard of or seen in the US?"

The doctor laughed and said, "Biggest of anything always seems to fascinate us, right Joe? Well, in post-Attica years, most prison systems have kept their census down to a maximum of twenty-two hundred inmates in any one prison for reasons of safety and better management of the inmate population. When considering maximum-security prisons, it is truly amazing to realize that Jackson Prison, just seventy miles outside of Detroit, Michigan, has been the largest single incarceration facility in America, with seven thousand inmates. With such a massive population, it was necessary to have all the agencies within the prison, including parole, medical, corrections counselors, mental health, volunteer services, and religious clergy, all working together, and collaborating effectively. One of the difficult challenges for correctional staff is being consistent in their approach and in their expectations of inmates and inmate-patients, in order to accomplish the goals of the mission in any corrections setting."

Lou Schultz then asked, "Are there many real benefits that cons—I mean inmates—can receive in prison? It seems all people talk about is cruelty, violence, and mayhem."

Doctor Barilla really enjoyed putting the rarely heard positive spin on life in prison.

"Contrary to many popular opinions about incarceration being cruel and unusual punishment, it seems that there are many overlooked positive benefits for incarcerated individuals. For example, the old saying, 'three hots and a cot,' reflects three decent meals a day and a comfortable sleeping arrangement. Many inmates benefit from taking advantage of exercise opportunities and become more physically fit than they were in the free community. When necessary, they can avail themselves of medical services, psychiatric services, drug and alcohol programs, religious/spiritual services, vocational programs, and numerous educational programs. They are offered pre-release services when approaching separation from incarceration, and those inmates who maintain positive disciplinary records become eligible for placement in the honor block, a special residence for those who earn it. The honor block, unlike the nine foot by eight foot cell in regular cell blocks, is a nine foot by twelve foot area with an unlocked door that remains open all day. Inmates in this block have their own washer and dryer right on the cellblock, unlimited access to a color television, and a lot of other privileges as long as they maintain a clean disciplinary record. For those inmates who are married who live anywhere in general population with good behavior, there are conjugal visits with loved ones. Such visits last for thirty hours in a trailer just outside the main buildings but still within the thirty-foot wall enclosure surrounding the prison. The daily routines for all of these inmates require personal responsibility and good citizenship within the corrections community."

The doctor anticipated questions about mentally and emotionally challenged inmate-patients.

"For those inmates who are living at a lower level of competence, the prison also has programs for managing their lives. Under the Academic Vocational Program, there is what is known as daycare, which normally has about fifty inmate-patients who are chronically mentally ill but are somewhat functional—at times much more so than at others—and some get better over time and are discharged into the general prison population. Almost all of them are on some kind of psychiatric medication and are kept busy in a lot of helpful programs including sports, recreational therapy, and occupational therapy.

"One program for those who are intellectually challenged is the simple setting of the time on a clock, or the hour to be awakened on an alarm clock, because some people, believe it or not, have never done even that small task. On occasion, some of these special inmates intermingle with the general population for various activities, even work assignments they can handle. The problem is that, although some of the regular inmates are pretty decent toward these challenged inmates-patients, there are a number of others who are predatory. Those predatory inmates have to be under a constant surveillance by all staff because there have been nasty con men who would take advantage of these inmate-patients in many ways. It is inspiring to see the variety and the range of services that are provided in the context of the maximum-security prison. It is something to be proud of in that it has come a long way from the very primitive warehousing and simply keeping an eye on inmates sitting off in a corner or laying on the floor doing nothing to an attempt to give challenged inmate-patients some type of stimulating, normal activities.

"Although there has been progress in these areas, there still is a long way to go. Some critics of the numerous benefits available to inmates have cynically referred to inmates as 'citizens' because they seem to have as many or more rights and privileges than law-abiding citizens in the free community. I must confess, that thought occurred to me at times, especially when sociopathic inmates despise and reject programs—which is their right—that might otherwise move them toward some measure of rehabilitation."

Rachel McGee, a nursing student taking this required psychology class, offered, "What was the prison environment like when AIDS came into the picture? Wasn't it in the late seventies or early eighties?"

"Yes it was, Rachel, and it was a scary challenge for all personnel and inmates in our prison. This was a dread disease that came to light when inmates began to show the final symptoms of pneumonia and cancer, and then began to die very quickly, as did many people with AIDS in the free community. Those who were working in the penitentiary, whether correctional or civilian staff or medical staff, were very nervous about not understanding the cause of this disease, how this disease was transmitted, and how contagious it was. Consequently, everyone feared for their lives. It was not unusual for physicians who entered an inmate's cell, who was known to have contracted AIDS, not want to shake hands with the inmate, let alone touch them, even while wearing rubber gloves. It was especially frightening because the staff did not know if such an inmate's bite, spit, urine, or just physical contact could result in someone contracting AIDS from the inmate. Inmates sometimes would take advantage of this situation by threatening to spit on people, to bite people, or to throw urine on them, in order to get their own way, or in order to instill fear in all those who had to deal with them. It was also discovered that a few inmates with AIDS exhibited neurological symptoms first, and became very problematic with their gait—the way they walked They were acting and talking like schizophrenic patients—very weird and off the wall—so it took a while to find out that the staff was dealing with AIDS Dementia Complex in those cases. All that was known about AIDS in those early years was what had been termed the 4-H Club, because the categories, or the areas, in which AIDS presented itself mostly among inmates were: Heroin users, Homosexuals, Hemophiliacs, and in a disproportionate number of Haitians."

The doctor asked his class, "What is it like to work in an environment such as this?"

Then, he answered his own question, "It really takes a special kind of person, one who has a unique understanding of, and an ability to cope with, the challenges of dealing with persons who must live in a structured and restricted setting. If one has consistent fear, claustrophobia, or abhorrence of violence and primitive behavior, it would be very difficult for that individual to work in such an environment. If any staff member marks a calendar every day, waiting for retirement to come in, let's say, eighteen years, seven months, and three days, in the same way as some inmates do waiting for their time to get out of prison—the final day of their sentence—then, this is not the right place for such a person. Inevitably, experience has shown that burnout and severe stress are the likely outcomes for such persons dealing with this kind of stress.

"One thing that mental-health personnel must keep in mind in the prison is that there is a wire system—namely the way information gets around—that is incredible among inmate networks. Inmates come to know each of those who work in the prison and his or her life as an employee better than could ever be imagined. They can sense things in people, especially any fear one might have, even if that person tries not to show it. And they are very resourceful in many ways in lockup, including fashioning unusual weapons. This is reality.

"Lastly, it is extremely important for correctional personnel, including mental- health staff, to have a sense of humor in one's repertoire of skills in order to pursue a mission in this kind of environment. For example, one might ponder why the bestselling product in the prison commissary is Vaseline."

These are just the basics Dr. Barilla discovered in dealing with the culture and life in a maximum-security prison. This is the real deal, what the inmates would call being "on the real side," meaning what the *real* truth is or what is really going on. So, the real deal on the real side.

CHAPTER 2

THE ETERNAL FLAME:
THE CHALLENGES OF CRISIS
INTERVENTION

As was often the case, the mental-health staff would get word that one of the inmate-patients was acting out of sorts or showing signs of mental instability. One morning, the word came down from G-Block correctional staff in Centerville Correctional Facility that Mahmoud Sharraf was seriously agitated and acting extremely threatening and bizarre. G-Block had a reputation for housing trouble-making inmates, and the block was called "Nairobi" by inmates and staff alike. The lead block officer, Ken Hutchinson, urged mental-health staff to intervene as soon as possible because the situation was critical in his opinion.

Ken was an excellent leader of his men, and he commanded respect from inmates as well. He also happened to be a student in Doctor Barilla's psychology class at Concord College, where he was also an excellent learner. The officer staff felt that Mahmoud was imminently dangerous to himself and others. The key words "clear, imminent, and dangerous" get the psychiatric staff moving fast. Mahmoud was part African-American and part Arab. He had a lengthy history of mental and emotional illness in which he experienced frequent episodes of psychosis and intermittent violent behavior.

Mahmoud was doing time after having been in and out of the prison psychiatric service and in and out of psychiatric inpatient service in a security-treatment hospital several times. Currently, he was incarcerated for murder, whereas on past occasions, he had served time for assault and battery episodes in which he had attacked and seriously injured people under the influence of drugs.

His murder charge was the result of a Metro Cab driver discovering that Mahmoud had pieces of a human body in a plastic bag, which he had carried with him when he hailed the cab to pick him up. The cabbie turned him in after calling the police in a furtive way when Mahmoud instructed the cab driver to stop at a remote section of the Patriot River, where he was going to dump the body. Mahmoud was now locked up for the duration of his time, probably for the rest of his natural life.

Mahmoud's condition on the day of this alarm summons necessitated, according to corrections policy, that the efforts of several disciplines within the prison first be utilized to solve this crisis before activating the Corrections Emergency Response Team (CERT). The involvement of the CERT most always meant the forcible extraction of an inmate from his cell and the shackling of that inmate before bringing him to "the Box," which was the disciplinary Special Housing Unit or SHU, or to a secure cell for mental-health observation, in the mental health "satellite" unit within the prison. Since Mahmoud had at various times claimed to be Catholic and Muslim, the Catholic priest and the inmate Muslim Imams were summoned to the scene. Additionally, members of the psychiatric team responded to the crisis.

With exceptional caution and guidance from correctional staff, each discipline, in turn, approached Mahmoud's cell in an attempt to resolve his crisis without physical force or violence. Unfortunately, with his bare hands, this large, intimidating brute had already physically destroyed and crushed the ceramic toilet and sink in his cell, while throwing the many broken pieces down from his third-tier enclosure, showering all three tiers as shards landed on the third tier, the second tier, and the first tier, in descending order. The entire cell block was closed down in anticipation of this intervention.

Mahmoud had blockaded the entrance to his cell with his metal bedspring. He was draped in bed sheets around his head and torso while proclaiming himself to be some kind of sheik. He was bleeding profusely from wounds on his hands and feet caused by the slivers of porcelain all around him. His menacing demeanor and wild facial expressions conveyed a message of murder and mayhem.

A member of each discipline cautiously approached his cell beginning with the inmate Imams who claimed to be the Muslim leaders in this facility.

They offered a few kind words of deference to Mahmoud, but his response to them was, "Step off, you motherfuckin' Niggers!"

For clarification, the use of the term "step off" means an inmate wants somebody to go away and/or just leave them alone.

Next came the venerable, long-term facility priest, Father Sean O'Leary, who barely uttered a few words of empathy and concern, to which Mahmoud screamed out, "Father, you can suck my dick!"

After that outburst, Father O'Leary wisely backed away mumbling, "I don't think I can help Mahmoud at this time."

Then, Dr. Hadjid stepped up to the cell. He had often ingratiated himself to Mahmoud in calm, therapeutic sessions by saying, "I am Muslim, too." Dr. Hadjid said he would give it a try, and he pleaded with Mahmoud to take his prescribed medication and to allow the psychiatric team to stabilize his condition as they had done many times in the past. Mahmoud leaned forward in his cell, almost as if listening appreciatively to Dr. Hadjid's genuine concern.

Mahmoud then exclaimed, "You know what, Dr. Hadjid? I'd like to fuck your mother."

Obviously, spiritual and healthcare interventions were not enough to calm the storm. The CERT immediately intervened and quickly, professionally, subdued Mahmoud without harm to the inmate-patient or to any correctional staff. The dutiful psychiatric nurse was standing by and quickly administered fifty milligrams of Thorazine intramuscularly in the right buttock. Within seconds, Mahmoud became docile and then unconscious. He was loaded onto a large, flat, laundry cart and wheeled away to the prison elevator while being escorted by correctional and psychiatric personnel.

As the team waited for the elevator, Dr. Hadjid took his pipe out of his pocket, lit it, and then leaned over and calmly stated to the unconscious Mahmoud, "I'd like to see you fuck my mother now."

Mahmoud was moved into psychiatric observation with continued proper medication and, within twenty-four hours, he was transported to the security-treatment hospital via an emergency commitment.

*****

Although not typically this serious, these are the type of crises that are part of the mental-health care of inmate-patients in a maximum-security prison. At times, when madness appears to be the order of the day, humor, as an ingredient of the intervention, can lend a measure of sanity to the providers.

In most instances, inmates, once they are incarcerated, once they get into a routine, start going to school, get a job in the prison, and see family on regular visits, they really do want to do their time and go home. They don't want to get into any pickle or to get into any serious disciplinary problems that will prolong their sentence and make it difficult to go home.

In many state prisons, they have what are called indeterminate sentences. Unlike the federal prisons, where a convicted felon gets a sentence and then must serve the entirety of that sentence, most state prisons have a parole system. If a convicted felon gets sentenced to a period of time, he can be eligible for early release under what is called a "zip bid." He can, if he has maintained good behavior, ask to come before the parole board to see if they will release him before his full sentence has been completed. In this case, if an inmate had been sentenced to seven years in prison, but has had good behavior, he can come before the parole board and may be allowed to leave after five years, for example, with two years of parole, which will satisfy the total seven-year sentence. During that two-year period that he is out on the street, he must report to a parole officer on a monthly basis as to his place of residence and place of work. If he violates these rules or is arrested for any reason, he will be sent back to prison to complete the remaining years of his original sentence. One must keep in mind, by the way, that prisons are for people who commit felonies. Jails are for people who commit misdemeanors or lesser crimes. The maximum stay in jail is 364 days, what inmates call a bullet, just one day under a year. Any time requiring a stay of a year or more is to be served in a prison setting.

The following includes information that is vital to understand by anyone who prepares to enter into the fascinating world of the mind and the challenges of intervening on behalf of those with mental illnesses. There's a theory that tries to link mental illness exclusively to chemical-imbalance disorders. Not all professionals in medicine and in mental health agree with this because that requires one to believe, among other things, that the mind is the brain and the brain is the mind. This involves a great philosophical and neuroscience debate because there are other professionals who see these two phenomena as two separate entities. There are psychiatrists who medicinally treat people with mental illnesses believing that the brain's biochemical malfunction is the sole cause for the patient's disturbed behavior. However, there are psychologists and social workers who diagnose the patient on the basis of cognitive distortions being the root cause of emotional illness, and treat with consequences— reward versus punishment—following the behaviors of the patient. This is called behavioral therapy. Most non-physician clinicians also believe in cognitive theory and therapy, discerning how thinking impacts emotions and behaviors as well as altering neurotransmitter functioning. Sometimes, these diagnoses by either side can be impulsive, in which case the professional jumps too quickly to a conclusion about a diagnosis without adequate consideration of alternative explanations.

In a study at Stanford University, Dr. David Rosenhan, a psychologist, created a research experiment that sent participants to twelve different hospitals in five different states at different times, with the intent of gauging the effectiveness of diagnosis. The eight people who were sent out included a psychology graduate student in his twenties, a pediatrician, a psychiatrist, a painter, and a housewife—three women and five men in all. They were instructed to go to the psychiatric emergency room, give a false name and job history when speaking to the admissions staff (to protect their future health and employment records), and told the receiving professionals only one symptom, that they were hearing voices. This study was entitled, "On Being Sane in Insane Places." Its purpose was to challenge a classification system created in the 1950s, when it was believed that abnormal behavior was the result of a medical illness. The widely used classification system was codified in the *Diagnostic and Statistical Manual of Mental Disorders*, a medical-model approach that attempted to codify all psychiatric disorders. Rosenhan's study was an attempt to demonstrate that the *DSM* was often unreliable as a clinical tool.

Each of the eight research subjects went to a hospital and said that he or she was hearing voices—they were all admitted to in-patient psychiatric care. They were committed to the hospital's psychiatric ward and diagnosed schizophrenic, even though, after being admitted, the pseudo-patients stopped simulating any symptoms of abnormality and they stopped claiming that they heard voices. The pseudo-patients normal behaviors were seen as aspects of their supposed illness. The pseudo-patients secretly kept written records of how the ward as a whole operated, as well as how they personally were treated. When it became clear that no one was concerned about the note taking, they continued to do it more openly. And even when the pseudo-patients who were faking mental illness told the staff, "I don't hear voices anymore," they were still kept in the psychiatric hospital.

The staff could not tell that they were faking. Guess who could? The truly psychotic patients on the ward in the hospital knew that these pseudo-patients were faking the symptoms by their claim of hearing voices. That is pretty scary, although comical.

Some actual patients voiced their suspicions very vigorously by stating, "You're not crazy. You're a journalist or a professor. You're checking up on the hospital."

When the pseudo-patients were finally released, they were discharged with a diagnosis of "schizophrenia in remission." Rosenhan noted that the experience of hospitalization for the pseudo-patients was one of depersonalization and powerlessness. Also, from the notes that were taken, it was revealed that some of the ward orderlies were brutal to patients in full view of other patients but would stop the offensive behavior as soon as another staff member approached.

It was estimated that the pseudo-patients were given a total of twenty-one hundred medication tablets, although only two were swallowed. The rest were either pocketed or flushed down the toilet by the pseudo-patients.

Finally, the records from the note-taking revealed that the nurses stayed in their ward offices about 90 percent of the time, and the number of times medical and psychiatric staff came into the ward and the amount of time spent with psychiatrists, psychologists, registrars, and so forth, on average, was under seven minutes a day. One comical conclusion that came out as a result of the study was the comment, "If you talk to God, you are praying. If God talks to you, you have schizophrenia." This became a published study and was designed to encourage professionals to be more cautious about how they diagnose and use pathological labels that they give to patients.

Dr. Barilla recalled, during his early years of study before coming to Martinsville, the influence of a professor in learning theory, which is like behavior theory, with its principles of positive reinforcement and punishment. The professor was a brilliant Korean fellow who had also been a sergeant in the South Korean army during the Korean conflict.

He used to say to all of his clinical students as they would go through his mandated class as part of their doctoral program, "Why in the hell don't you leave those troubled people alone? Why do you have to put a label on them that they are going to carry with them for the rest of their life? It is not fair. It is not right. Just let them be. If they're not harming anybody, why do you do that?"

Doctor Barilla never forgot that. It has since always been a guide for Dr. Barilla in terms of being cautious in his career when making a decision about an appropriate diagnosis.

The commentary of that Korean professor seems to be supported by a second study made by Rosenhan, which was a sequel to his earlier study. In this follow-up study, which was accomplished at a teaching and research hospital some months following the earlier Rosenhan experiment, everyone at the hospital was aware of the results of that previous experiment. However, the psychiatric staff was told that during the next three months, one or more pseudo-patients would attempt to be admitted into their hospital. Their job was to rate each patient as to the likelihood of them being a pseudo-patient or a real patient.

In the final analysis, of the 193 patients judged, 41 were confidently believed to be pseudo-patients by at least one staff member. Twenty-three were suspected of being pseudo-patients by one psychiatrist, and 19 were suspected of being pseudo-patients by one psychiatrist and one other staff member.

In actuality there were *no* pseudo-patients.

Rosenhan claimed that the studies demonstrated that psychiatrists cannot reliably tell the differences between the people who are psychotic and those who are not psychotic. The first experiment illustrated a failure to accurately detect sanity, and the secondary study demonstrated a failure to accurately detect insanity. It should be noted here that "insanity" is actually a legal term but often used interchangeably with "psychotic," a mental-health term.

*****

In a maximum-security prison, the psychiatric nurses and the correction officers, on the front line in service to forensic mental-health care, are the ones who are so very crucial to the smooth operation of the facility in terms of supervising, observing, and establishing rapport with inmate-patients. They are crucial because these nurses see the inmate-patients more than other health professionals. They also administer the medication, either in the unit clinic or down in the cell blocks, however many times a day that needs to be done. And the officers live with the inmate-patients and are in charge of managing them on eight-hour shifts, 24-7.

If professional staff, such as doctors or psychiatrists or psychologists, are arrogant or condescending to uniformed officers, they forfeit the opportunity to get crucial feedback from the COs about inmate-patients' behavior.

If treated like dirt, the COs will usually say, "Hey, screw that arrogant doctor. We're not gonna tell him shit! We're not gonna to tell him anything about the real deal with this inmate in the cell block."

In such a situation, the truth of inmate-patients' statements to clinicians—such as claims that they are psychotic and hearing voices, when, in fact, the COs see them twenty-four hours a day and know better—would go unreported by CO staff. Thus, the inmate-patients might be assumed to be abnormal on the cell blocks and might have to be evaluated when they come to mental health for an interview. The evaluation would then be missing valuable information about the inmate-patient's everyday functioning. Some COs see that as a vengeful lesson to arrogant professionals. Furthermore. the missing information decreases the likelihood of an accurate diagnosis, considering that it is also true that most inmate-patients are not completely truthful.

The lesson here is that COs and all prison personnel need to be viewed and treated as valuable members of the collective team that manages inmate-patients in a maximum-security prison.

A famous psychologist, Dr. Stanton Samenow, author of *Inside the Criminal Mind,* has really done a lot to help professionals and students understand the difficult business of sociopathy—the antisocial personality disorder—especially in the context of treatment in mental health. He basically said that if one of these sociopaths tells you something, and you listen and understand what they're saying but you disagree with their point of view, they say you don't understand them. It is because you disagree with them that they feel you don't understand them—in their opinion they are misunderstood and unfairly treated because you disagree. So, if they have some irrational justification for punching a guy in the nose or committing robbery or abusing somebody and they, in their own minds, feel justified in what they did and they do not feel that it was some kind of impropriety—they really feel strongly that you just don't understand them. That is an important example of the distorted thinking process that is present in the cognitive functioning in most of these character-disordered perpetrators, even those with some form of Axis I mental illness.

Chapter 3

From the Pristine to Purgatorial: The Making of a Forensic Clinician

Dr. Barilla's first experience as a psychologist was at Henry Ford Hospital in Detroit, Michigan. This was before the doctor became involved with the prison mental-health system. The Henry Ford Hospital was a pristine setting, both physically and professionally. It had multidisciplinary teams. All healthcare staff wore three-quarter length white coats. There were carpeted hallways, and everyone had an office with a sign that said **DO NOT DISTURB** for use when the mental-health professionals had patients in their offices for counseling. The staff could go across the hallway and watch the neurology team do an EEG or other medical procedures. The team included specialists in psychiatry, neurology, neurosurgery, psychology, and social work, all on the same floor. It was very stimulating professionally.

The hospital even had an honest-to-goodness Austrian psychiatric chief, Dr. Franz Von Hitz, who, in his thick Austrian accent, used to pronounce "schizophrenic" like, "shitsophrenic," and it was always amusing to listen to him cite that diagnosis. And there were a lot of learning experiences there, especially with journal clubs. That was when every member of the professional team discussed his or her views and findings about a particular patient. Then, after hearing each other, staff would invite that patient in, and interview the patient together, being very supportive and empathetic with them. The psychiatric team used to have guest speakers from different areas, and Dr. Barilla brought in a few speakers from his alma mater, the University of Detroit, where he had received his master's degree in psychology.

The hospital had its own research team, which did different kinds of health research, involving a whole range of inpatient/outpatient care, and which generated a number of very informative reports. Being a participant in many professional activities, Dr. Barilla got to know everyone pretty well. There was one social worker, Phyllis Jones, in particular who, for some reason, decided to flood the top of his desk with literature from NOW, the National Organization of Women. This happened a lot.

Doctor Barilla pretended not to know who sent it, and he would say, "Well, Phyllis, I wonder where that came from?"

She would respond, "I don't know, but you should read it. You should find out about women."

So, one day, the doctor decided to bust her butt, and he went up to the twelfth floor of the hospital where the medical library was situated, and, lo and behold, he found a volume of Shakespeare's works—all thirty-seven major plays and all of Shakespeare's poetry. Doctor Barilla took the soliloquy out from *The Taming of the Shrew*, in which the shrew, Katrina, after she was tamed by Petruchio, does a complete 180-degree turnaround on her attitude toward men. Previously, men had feared Katrina, and she regularly disrespected them. Then, she gives this speech to her lady friends admonishing them to be in servitude and obey every command from their magnificent husbands. It is one funny tale. So Doctor Barilla left that on the desk of his colleague, the social worker. Phyllis laughed hysterically and never brought any more NOW literature into his office.

Dr. Barilla learned early in his career at Henry Ford Hospital how certain people tried to use the mental-health system to achieve selfish, unethical goals. A perfect example was the son and daughter-in-law of an aging, retired woman school teacher, who was showing early signs of dementia. The couple was trying to get Dr. Barilla to produce mental-health reports to indicate that the mother, Gertrude Schaeffer, was incompetent to manage her financial affairs. The son's goal was to gain access to and complete control of all his mother's assets, despite the absence of any convincing evidence to support the alleged incompetence. Dr. Barilla documented the son's unethical behavior in Gertrude's medical chart, chastised the son and daughter-in-law, and entered his professional opinion in Gertrude's chart that she was competent to manage her own affairs, even though the patient was working through a period of depression at that time.

There were many other notable patients at Henry Ford Hospital in Dr. Barilla's short tenure there. Perhaps the most unusual case was the psychotic, suicidal, adult daughter of a famous Grand Rapids lawyer, Samuel Lippert. The daughter, Gail, was psychiatrically hospitalized after her latest failed suicide attempt, a sailor dive off an overpass onto a major highway which ran through the city of Detroit. Her skull was cracked in numerous places, and after several weeks of eating poorly during her recovery and treatment, she lost 40 percent of her body weight. She was consistently on IV treatment for sustenance. She had numerous severe mental and emotional problems, such that she was unable to cooperate in psychological testing or psychotherapy sessions. Medications and occasional shock therapy were the only mental-health treatment modalities of any value for this tragic patient.

It also happened that Gail's older sister, Julie, was a character-disordered woman who plotted terror against government agencies and was imprisoned for skyjacking a commercial airliner and attempting to take the plane to Cuba. She had been subdued by federal marshals who posed as civilian passengers, and she was subsequently brought to justice in federal court. The wealthy parents of these troubled ladies lavished material goods upon them, which had created an exaggerated sense of entitlement and immunity from societal rules—without parental attention to boundaries, character development, and personal responsibility. The calamity and chaos in the lives of these disturbed sisters was understandable, given their dysfunctional developmental histories and incompetent parents.

After Dr. Barilla left the Henry Ford Hospital and eventually went to work in a maximum-security prison, he came to realize that the hospital was probably the first and last clinic in his career to have a fully staffed multidisciplinary team treating patients who were motivated for treatment and who probably had to pay big bucks to receive professional services.

After working nearly eight months at the hospital, Doctor Barilla made a career change by taking a position in the psychiatric clinic for the criminal court in Detroit, Michigan. It was a challenging job in which the mental-health staff evaluated detainees— county-jail inmates who were facing trial and sentencing. Some detainees who the clinicians saw had already been placed on probation. Dr. Barilla and his colleagues would see them in group therapy and individual therapy as outpatients. And, interestingly, the judges of Recorders' Court mandated that these clinicians make recommendations of detainees that they evaluated, as to whether they should be sent to prison or to be let out on probation. Weighty responsibility! Dr. Barilla was really surprised at that. So he, along with his medical and mental-health group, administered a variety of intelligence and personality tests, interviewed the detainees, and then put the report together to be presented to the respective judges of the Recorders' Court.

The chief psychiatrist, Dr. Albert Forman, was a man with a goatee and a way of looking at patients and other people with one eye always squinting. So Dr. Barilla dubbed him Dr. Svengali. On one occasion, Dr. Forman dealt with a detainee who was a goofy character in very bizarre clothing, who wore a Boy Scout belt to hold his pants up. So, when interviewing the patient, Dr. Forman put him up against the wall and just stared at him. The patient got really nervous.

Finally, Dr. Forman said, "I just have one question. Where did you get that Boy Scout belt?"

With that, the patient became even more nervous and defensive. He didn't know what was going on or how to handle it, and staff who witnessed this scene chuckled at the patient.

They finally said, "It's okay. We're just having a little fun with you."

They finished the evaluation, and the young man went on his way.

As an added note of interest, Dr. Forman used to say, "When you interview a detainee and, after twenty minutes you like him, that detainee is a sociopath!"

*****

At Recorders' Court there was a judge, named Juan Velasquez, who was a man of questionable character himself. He seemed quite paranoid about the establishment and the police. Every day, the court security officers had to perform the ritual of remotely starting his car out in the parking lot, after the judge's working day, because of his fear that a bomb might have been planted in retaliation by some of the alleged perpetrators who entered his court. One never knew what would come out of his mouth. He had a habit of saying controversial things to the press, sometimes insulting the judicial system, implying negative things about his own colleagues, and clearly ridiculing or condemning the police and others in the field of law enforcement.

At the same time in Detroit, there was a policeman named Charlie Kronowski, who, as a rookie cop, had seen his partner get gunned down by Black Panthers in the Bethel church incident. So Charlie decided to go undercover in the streets of Detroit to try to bust criminals and reduce the crime epidemic that was plaguing the city. He posed as a drug user and a potential customer to whom dealers could sell drugs, and he got into some really tough gun battles and had been known to have shot eight or ten criminals as a result of these gunfights in the streets of Detroit. Detroit has had a reputation of being like a war zone sometimes.

Then one day, Kronowski was summoned to court where a black lawyer, Charles Dunbar, was trying to make a case for his client in front of Judge Velasquez. By the way, Judge Velasquez always carried a little revolver under his robe, in his belt. So, here in court, along with Dr. Barilla, were all these witnesses for both the defense and the prosecution. This lawyer, Dunbar, was trying to embarrass Office Charlie Kronowski, who was sitting on the witness stand. The lawyer, suddenly surprised everyone, pulled out a fake gun, and began waving it in the direction of Kronowski, who, responding to his training and experience, pulled out two loaded weapons and shot the lawyer dead, right in the courtroom. Judge Velasquez sank to the floor and crawled to the back door to get out of the courtroom, while everybody in the whole courtroom hit the deck.

Meanwhile, Officer Kronowski went over to make sure that the lawyer was not going to shoot anybody with what the policeman thought was a real gun.

Kronowski got into no trouble for this incident, and the lawyer whose theatrics in order to prove a point to the judge and jury backfired, obviously made a very ill-advised mistake in pulling this gun that looked very real. So Velasquez got himself a really bad reputation for that occurrence in his courtroom, and he did not stay on the bench very long. The story made the headlines and was featured in some of the national magazines.

*****

Another court-clinic experience involved a female psychiatrist and her husband psychiatrist, both of whom had been family practice physicians and had decided to get the appropriate training and move into the field of psychiatry. Apparently, they both took a residency of some kind and then began working in the Criminal Court in Detroit. The lady, Dr. Ann Miller, was a nice person, but she began to exhibit some significantly misguided benevolence, which Dr. Barilla noticed during group therapy in which she and Dr. Barilla worked together as group co-therapists. For example, when a probationer in the group complained that he did not have enough bus money to get home and he was having a hard time financially. These were outpatient probationers coming to the clinic for therapy. So Dr. Ann Miller reached into her purse and pulled out a ten-dollar bill and gave it to the patient. Well, as could be expected, in subsequent weeks, two or three more times, someone in the group would come up with an equally sad story, and Dr. Miller would once again pull out money and give it to the probationer in front of everyone else. Then, Dr. Barilla talked to the clinic director about that, and the director, in turn, talked to Dr. Miller and told her that she had to stop doing that kind of behavior. She disagreed, but went along with the program, as far as anyone could tell.

Then again, there was this problem: Dr. Miller refused to co-sign reports that she and Dr. Barilla had to produce together. It was protocol for all the psychologists to team up with one of the psychiatrists and give their reports as a combined account that would, when completed, go to the judges for their examination. The hang up here was that Dr. Miller, for example, might take exception to the word "maladaptive" if Dr. Barilla used that description in his analysis of a patient. The word simply translates as someone who exhibits criminal behavior, an element in that patient's make-up that Dr. Barilla was attempting to correct. But if Dr. Miller saw that word "maladaptive," she would not co-sign the report because in her estimation, that language was much too strong for these "poor fellows" from out there in the underprivileged community. Therefore, in order to get a report completed and signed by a psychiatrist, the director of this clinic, who was a psychologist himself, tried to work things out by teaming Doctor Barilla up with another psychiatrist so that the report would finally have both signatures from the psychologist and psychiatrist examining the respective patient. One never knew what to expect, whether it be from a patient or from a doctor.

*****

At this point, there are two other issues that must be addressed, as they sometimes arise when dealing with those in the mental-health profession. The first one has been lightly touched on with the aforementioned example of how some clinicians, themselves, seem to be in need of counseling. There will be more about this to follow. The second issue is the fact that some people in this profession, as in many other professions, can be very arrogant and can practice in ways that one would have to wonder how it is allowed.

As an example, there was a psychiatrist, Dr. Morton Kramstein, who came to Detroit from Boston one time to attend one of the clinic meetings in the Recorders' Court clinic. He received a bit of notoriety during the time of the infamous Boston Strangler murders and had been quoted in the press along with other psychiatrists who thought they had some insight into the perpetrator's mind. Dr. Kramstein had a reputation for being good in physiognomy, the so-called science of reading faces and then being able to tell what a person is really like and what his or her character was like and even to predict his or her behavior. This guy was a really pompous ass and unbelievably arrogant and narcissistic. Although his reason for coming to this meeting was to give those clinicians on staff, as well as their invitees, some information relating to the Boston Strangler, he decided to jump right into this physiognomy routine.

He said to those who were gathered, "Go ahead. Pull out any file you have on any detainee or inmate, and I'll tell you all about him."

So the staff pulled out a file, and Dr. Kramstein looked at the inmate's picture and told everyone the patient's background, his supposed history, and his supposed current issues. His interpretation was all wrong! So the staff gave him another inmate's photo and he did exactly the same thing. No matter what photo was shown to Dr. Kramstein, the staff doctors had the factual information, and the visiting doctor screwed up everyone he "sight-analyzed." He really made a fool of himself.

The clinicians and guests who came in to listen to this "expert" turned to the staff clinicians and, shaking their heads, said in disgust, "Holy mackerel! Where did this guy come from?"

There is about as much science to physiognomy, with the exception of six basic facial expressions of certain emotions—happiness, surprise, anger, sadness, fear, and disgust—as there is to some other aspects of psychological analysis that should, in reality, be considered quackery. For example, phrenology is a pseudoscience that was very popular for centuries. It involves mapping twenty-seven human traits on a person's head, often referred to as "brain organs," and feeling areas of the head for bumps on the skull to determine strengths and weaknesses. These bumps were supposed to be the determining factors of a person's character. Notions of physiognomy go back at least to Aristotle's time, while phrenology is just several centuries old. It is good to know about some of the history of professional attempts to understand, predict, and change maladaptive thinking, feelings, and behavior, both past and present. However, these are examples of pseudoscience and are not utilized by reputable practitioners.

One further example is trephining, which is a process of boring holes into a person's head to release demons or evil spirits and also to prevent these evil spirits from entering into a person's mind. This practice goes back at least seven thousand years to the Stone Age and, reportedly, some strange folks in some parts of the world are still doing it today! There were probably three general techniques involved in trephining: scraping, drilling, and cutting. What is truly amazing is the fact that, although the operation was performed on men, women, and children, it was most often performed on adult males, and patients who underwent the operation had an impressive recovery rate. Considering the danger of severe bleeding, shock, brain edema, and infection, the achievements of such postoperative results suggest considerable skill and experience.

This bit of history has some importance because it is relevant to the previous belief, for centuries, that mental illness had a moral basis, even a Biblical basis, which held that demons had to be cast out. The practice of trephining was in a class with bloodletting, chaining to walls, hydrotherapy, violent beatings, and other inhumane methods intended to restrain, cleanse, and provide catharsis to the "possessed" individuals. Trephining might be viewed as the precursor to lobotomy (politely called "psychosurgery" in recent times), in which a surgeon would sever the nerves in the brain to relieve chronic backaches or agonizing headaches by first doing a leucotomy, which is the drilling of the holes in the skull to access the brain. Trephining may also be viewed as a precursor to exorcisms, the casting out of evil spirits mostly through the intervention by clergy. It is also worthy to note that shock therapy started several centuries ago and is still used today, albeit sparingly.

When one considers the history of treating the mentally ill, an interesting episode can be found in the Bethlehem Royal Hospital in London, England. During the eighteenth century, people went there to see the "lunatics." For a penny, one could peer into their cells, view the freaks of the "show of Bethlehem" and laugh at their antics. In 1814, there were 96,000 such visits! The lunatics were first called "patients" in 1700, and "curable" and "incurable" wards were opened several years later. In its earliest years, conditions were consistently dreadful, and the care amounted to little more than restraint. According to one report, there were thirty-one patients and the noise was "so hideous, so great, that they are more able to drive a man that hath his wits rather out of them." Even in more modern times—and that term is used with great caution—there were psychiatric hospitals that used antiquated methods of managing mentally-ill people. Chaining them to walls or hosing them down was still in their repertoire of treatment. There is some interesting research that was done to show how mental-health professionals also abuse the current system by sometimes giving a patient an unjustifiable, pathological diagnosis and, at times, being too quick to psychiatrically hospitalize certain patients.

*****

To conclude the cursory history of weird theories and primitive methods of treatment for mental illness and violence, reference needs to be made to the "miracle drugs," such as, Thorazine, Stelazine, Zoloft, Lithium, and a variety of other anti-psychotic, anti-anxiety, anti-hallucinogenic, and anti-depressant drugs that were discovered around the early 1950s. Along with the drugs, more effective modalities of psychotherapy, and greater understanding of the roles of neurotransmitters in the mental disease process, and more scientific classification of illnesses, were coming into the purview of mental-health clinicians. These things might be addressed in the context of seeing how far medicine has come. But has that much progress been made in treating mental illness and sociopathy?

Although these methods have, in most cases, replaced the need to use more forceful, restrictive kinds of management, psychiatric treatment still employs camisoles— straightjackets and restraining sheets (literally a canvas sheet used to tie a person's entire body to a bed)—when necessary. But one of the most humane interventions has been the "chemical restraint," the use of intramuscular injections to calm people down when they are wild or out of control. Again, despite the great scientific advances and humane treatment of mental/emotional illness, one still wonders about *efficacy* when one looks at the *outcomes* of all these efforts vis-à-vis the quality of life: more crime, more prisons, more mental illness and sociopathy, ad nauseam. It appears that all these disorders and related social problems continue to steadily increase nationally and globally!

*****

As Dr. Barilla thought back to the early days in his career, he often wished that he could have been exposed to teaching material that would have given him more realistic, unusual clinical encounters with patients in the field, especially in forensic work. As Dr. Barilla reflected upon so many of the things he witnessed, he could recall numerous incidents in which he played a part, and yet later wondered why he had not been made aware of such activities during his doctoral training. Upon further reflection, the doctor realized that his training did prepare him well for unpredictable and novel experiences.

Another lesson learned was that every therapeutic encounter is a unique experience, whatever the diagnosis might be. For example, one time, one of the detainee-patients he saw at Recorders' Court Clinic was a young man, Clint Johnson, who had walked about seven or eight miles in his bare feet in the middle of winter. In their session together, the patient told Doctor Barilla that he played Monopoly with God and he always beat God. Dr. Barilla figured he would have to get to know this guy because he must be brilliant. Now, to this day, the doctor does not know, looking back, if that young man really got the best of him with some drummed-up psychotic problem or possibly the delusion was real. Wow, the patient sure was bizarre!

All Doctor Barilla could think about was, *God, I never read about anything like that or heard anything like that in the ! ures in school,* about somebody playing Monopoly with God and beating Him at that game.

That was a valuable learning experience for Dr. Barilla. It was this pervasive thought that encouraged him to prepare this book, not only for those who will relate to what he has seen but also for those who are considering the field of psychology for their lifelong endeavor. With that in mind, the doctor continued to remember other experiences as well as his ever-developing perspective on what he practiced.

*****

In the Criminal Court, Doctor Barilla saw a lot of junkies and alcoholics from the streets as well as from the Detroit motor companies. The joke was, "Don't buy a car built on Monday, where people have major hangovers, or on Friday, where they are short-handed, because people bang in sick and go out to get an early start on the weekend drinking and drugging." It was tragic to see many of the previously poor people who had been in the South—both white and black—who moved to Detroit during the Second World War and began to work in the converted automobile factories that were producing military vehicles and machines. Most of these people stayed in Detroit after the war and had good jobs, were union people, and acquired pretty decent assets, as well as made a comfortable, secure life for themselves. But during the 1960s and 1970s, they often had trouble raising their children in that environment, and their offspring often had an anemic work ethic and some were antisocial in their behavior. So, when Dr. Barilla would see parents who came up the hard way and wanted to give their kids what they didn't have in their impoverished youth and wanted to shower them with material things, it sometimes didn't work out very well in terms of the development of their offspring.

One guy that Doctor Barilla remembered who was in the probation group, was a great example of how bad-habit patterns get stronger with antisocial behavior if they are not corrected early on. This was a young man who admitted he did over fifty burglaries before he actually got caught and did a short time in jail, followed by a period of probation. For the record, people who engage in antisocial behavior and are not caught, not punished, or are not confronted, actually are rewarded for that behavior and that particular behavior pattern. The habit gains strength over time. It was not until after the first fifty burglaries that this probationer was caught, so he enjoyed the rewards of his previous felonies, while not feeling much negative impact of the relatively light consequences. And it is hard to extinguish some habit patterns, especially when judges keep extending probation to somebody who commits a burglary, gets on probation, is busted again for burglary, and probation is extended.

What Dr. Barilla meant by this is: what is the deterrent here? Seemingly, the risk is worth it when inmates or detainees or criminal types know that nothing really bad is likely to happen, even if they are busted and convicted for a crime.

*****

Professional ethics is something else that can be an issue of concern when beginning professional practice in the field of psychology. People in medicine, people doing counseling, people in law enforcement, people in the clergy, people in teaching, people in politics, in fact, any one in a public arena or private practice can become victims or perpetrators of tainted ethics. For example, when Dr. Barilla was teaching college—he regularly taught a course in psychology as an adjunct at different colleges over many years—he found teaching to be very rewarding for him and quite a lot of fun.

Once in a while, he would encounter some admirer, a student of the opposite sex, usually a divorcee, who sat in the front row for every class. Her dresses seemed to get shorter and shorter with the passage of time, and she seemed to be revealing more and more of her anatomy. She always came up after class and would talk to the doctor as long as she could before he would leave the scene. Doctor Barilla used to tell students that, at the end of the semester, he would invite all of them up to see the Criminal Court Clinic, take them around, show them how it works, and what clinicians in his profession do there. Students are almost always fascinated with forensic psychology. So as the semester end approached, he invited the class to come and visit his clinic, and as it turned out, the female student in question was the only one who decided to accept the invitation.

Given her semester-long behavior, the doctor was a bit nervous. So he called on his bachelor, social-worker buddy, a great-big, red-bearded Irishman, John Kelly—who Doc called the Big Red Jesus—to join him for lunch. Dr. Barilla explained to John that he had a nice lady student coming up to see the clinic, and that he, the doctor, would like to excuse himself after lunch and get back to work. John agreed to help the doctor out so that Dr. Barilla could make a gracious getaway from his admiring student, and John might enjoy meeting an attractive, single lady.

Doctor Barilla recounted this simple tale to say that in private practice, or in any situation, when someone is in a position of authority, power, and trust, they may become the object of infatuation by those they come in contact with professionally. Professionals need to develop sound attitudinal and behavioral boundaries—usually taught thoroughly in graduate school—which they *never* violate under any circumstances! Aside from the all-important conviction a professional must have about professional ethics, a couple of useful fantasies, serving as a deterrent to ethics violation, might be, for example, envisioning a spouse waiting at home with divorce papers on the table—or one's professional license, with wings attached, flying away forever!

Chapter 4

In the Thick of It:
Meeting the Challenges with Zeal

Working in a maximum-security prison in Massachusetts is really where Dr. Barilla "made his bones" and gained lots of great experience, He came to view the difficult work as a challenge and, believe it or not, it was to him truly rewarding. It involved working in many different units in the general context of maximum-security, starting out in the hospital for the criminally insane and then working in a unit for acutely dangerous or acutely mentally ill young people who are, in the truest meaning of the words, difficult to manage.

The state was about to bring the full range of mental-health care into maximum-security prisons after the corrections system agreed to have the community mental-health model developed in those prisons by the Office of Mental Health. Dr. Barilla felt privileged and thrilled that he was there through all these exciting changes. He loved sharing, in retrospect, some of the highlights of that transition over several years.

He began to share the evolving history of mental-health care in prison, as well as his own experiences, in the warden's newly-instituted, bi-weekly, Thursday morning think-tank meetings. The warden wanted Dr. Barilla to facilitate discussions with leaders of all the disciplines in prison, to explain the mental-health mission, and to have all disciplines share feedback and coordinate all efforts in correctional care. It was especially important with the new system of delivering mental-health care within the maximum-security prison.

At the very first think-tank meeting, Dr. Barilla began:

"As I first started on my first job in a criminal mental-health hospital, I walked alone to my new psychiatric unit in the Martinsville State Hospital for the Criminally Insane, I heard increasingly loud, hostile voices. Unable to see anyone, I estimated maybe ten or twelve separate voices spewing insults, swear words, something about challenging each others' credentials? The language was choppy with incomplete sentences, like from inmates with foreign accents or maybe from a mentally retarded or emotionally disturbed ward?

"I thought, *How could a violent ward be placed so close to the inmate-patient cafeteria?*

"I had once read about psychologist, Milton Rokeach, at Ypsilanti State Hospital, conducting group therapy with three patients, each one proclaiming that he was Jesus Christ. Dr. Rokeach ultimately wrote a book entitled, *The Three Christs of Ypsilanti,* in which he described the lengthy, formidable task of doing therapy with those psychotic patients.

"I asked myself, *Do we have the Ten Holy Apostles of Martinsville behind the door of this scary, dangerous-sounding, violent ward?*

"After nervously pausing near this mysterious zone, I made my way through the cafeteria toward my new unit, with every intention of asking my experienced colleagues about the aggressive inmate-patients whose ranting and raving I just heard, but when I arrived at my unit on this second day of my orientation, I got lost in the greeting of my new colleagues, instruction about our unit programs, and my assigned responsibilities, and totally forgot about the question I wanted to pose.

"After a week of orientation, during which time I witnessed various inmate-patients in straitjackets, restraining sheets, on suicide watch, and some receiving forced medications, I finally remembered to ask someone about the scary ward I had encountered a few days earlier, which experience didn't seem unusual to me by that point.

"I asked a corrections officer, 'Is that a room where they lock up the out-of-control patients?'

"The CO said, 'No! That's the psychiatrists having their morning meeting!'

"So it was something to see all these professional doctors—from Poland, Turkey, India, South America, and a few Americans thrown in— in the midst of what purported to be a productive meeting of the minds. Many of them were on temporary licenses in the early days because the state could not always find licensed, competent people to work in these facilities. What must be understood is that, in later years, a few of the doctors who had all the credentials, the license, and the education, sometimes did things that were just as bizarre as those actions witnessed among the inmate-patients, in a few cases."

Bob Christopher, new corrections counselor, asked Dr. Barilla, "What kinds of danger to staff should we be aware of?"

The doctor came right back: "Very important question; we'll talk a lot about this issue on a regular basis. For example, it was in this setting, while in this hospital for the criminally insane, that a female psychologist, Anne Schroeder, was murdered in her Barrington apartment by an inmate-patient on leave because she had take up romantically with the sociopath. She had been dedicated to her work and her patients, but she let herself be taken in by this inmate-patient, who had previously been found incompetent to stand trial for his first murder and was at the time of Anne's killing allowed occasional furloughs.

"It was on one of these furloughs that he killed Anne. She was murdered the same way, under similar pretext, that he had murdered the woman that had gotten him into prison in the first place. The only difference being that the first woman was stabbed to death while Anne, on the other hand, was found on her bed, in her apartment, beaten severely and strangled to death with her stocking.

"The inmate-patient, Hector Rivera, a cold-blooded sociopath, later admitted to four murders in New York, Mexico City, and San Francisco. He fled to Argentina, his native country, after the police declared him to be the primary suspect and were looking for him.

"What needs not to be lost here is the unfortunate, foolish, unethical behaviors, by Anne Schroeder, which led to her brutal murder. In those days in Martinsville State Hospital, too many professionals lost track of appropriate boundaries in the name of treatment of mentally ill sociopaths, especially certain female staff with messianic tendencies. These are classic examples of mental-health professionals ignoring Axis II stuff, personality disorders, in favor of addressing only Axis I stuff, like depression, much of which is often fabricated by those sociopaths!"

Alicia Ford, a new nurse in the medical department, asked, "Why weren't the real bad guys sent to a regular prison? Did they want to be in a hospital with lots of crazy people?"

Dr. Barilla answered, "There were some advantages during those early years in being an inmate in a security-treatment hospital. A lot of inmate-patients would feign mental illness so that they could go there and live in a dormitory instead of a nine-foot by eight-foot crib, which describes a prison cell. They could have sex with their sweethearts in the visitation room by getting down under the tables that were covered with flowing tablecloths. They could get all kinds of medication to ease the unpleasantness of incarceration. They could avoid some of the harsh and dangerous stuff that goes on in prisons in general, not the least of which is some big, bad 'Bubba,' bending them over, with an intent to 'pack your fudge!'

"In those days, sometimes one would see corrections officers pouring liquid Thorazine into a drinking glass to give to these inmate-patients, to calm them down. There was a lot of self-mutilation going on when the inmate-patients were told that they were going to be discharged to prison, because they did not want to go. Often, they would cut their arms, cut their neck, do all kinds of shenanigans or talk about hearing voices out of the light bulbs, and crazy behavior like that.

"And, in that setting, I distinctly remember one particular inmate-patient who was a very despondent guy, generally depressed, who cut both of his forearms to the bone. He then went into the urinals in the bathroom, which had these barriers between them and, like doing isometric exercises, he pushed against both barriers (to his right and to his left) so that he could force the blood out of his arms more quickly. He was caught and pulled from the bloody mess and taken to the nurses' station where one of the psychiatrists began sewing him up. It was quite a sight to see different layers of skin and flesh all the way down to the bone. The staff was standing there holding the inmate in place, with the doctor sewing him up, and this big correction officer, Hank Engel, who was helping to keep the inmate-patient still. Suddenly, Hank turned real pale and leaned against the wall and started sliding down to the floor. I reached under the CO's forearms and held him up and brought him over to a chair. Staff got the job done and then put this young inmate-patient on a suicide watch.

"Eventually, we sent him to the medical-hospital unit where they could treat him medically and also watch him constantly to prevent any future attempts at suicide. We continued to psychiatrically medicate the patient in that setting. But, unfortunately, this was an inmate-patient who ultimately left prison, went back home to Boston somewhere, and succeeded in killing himself out there in the street. This was another teaching experience that, despite our best efforts, we can't save everyone!"

A new psychiatrist, Dr. Woo, asked, "Doc B., can you address what resources we have for inmates and inmate-patients with special needs?"

The doctor thought a minute and said, "In the unit for acutely disturbed young men, they also had other specialty cases, such as the elderly, the handicapped, and the retarded. In this particular unit for the acutely disturbed, they had a lot of young inmates who really had acting-out problems. The good thing is that the medical and mental-health staffs had real secure, controlled units and could keep these inmate-patients on a positive path. We sometimes used restraint and seclusion and appropriate medications. It didn't take long for inmate-patients with sociopathic traits to get the picture.

"This was an example where vicarious learning is powerful, where one inmate sees what is happening to someone else, and he figures, 'Holy shit! I don't think I wanna' do that behavior because I don't want that consequence!' Likewise, if an inmate-patient sees another patient receiving a positive consequence from certain behaviors, it is more likely that the others will engage in the rewarded behavior. It can be very effective and can motivate a person in a positive direction. Again, we believed that all clinical interventions were necessary and were delivered as humanely as possible, in a very active, sometimes violent atmosphere."

Dr. Barilla offered another example: "At one time, there was an inmate who was attempting to hang himself, and he was caught in time, cut down, and then went into *status epilepticus*, which is quite a sight to see. That inmate, who had nearly hung himself, was turning blue in the face while having a true epileptic seizure. The seizure activity can go on for a considerably lengthy period of time, depending on the rapidity of the intervention. In this case, the medical staff injected him with Valium or some other sedative to stabilize him. The inmate was then transferred from the acute unit to the security psychiatric hospital. Worthy of note here is that nearly all successful suicides in prison are done by hanging. Typically, the victim ties one end of a sheet or belt or some rope-like device around a cell bar or some metal protrusion and the other end of that device is tied around his neck. Then he slowly slides down against the wall into a state of lethal strangulation. It usually takes four to five minutes for the inmate to expire!"

The doctor continued: "It was in the unit for the acutely disturbed that I met and worked with another psychiatric colleague, a real character, Dr. Hans Van Yoder. He was born in Central Europe and was an intelligent but humorless, distant kind of colleague. He was short in stature, slight of build, and had some effeminate characteristics, including his gait. He regularly ground his teeth in a closed-mouth fashion, like someone with Temporomandibular Joint Syndrome. He often appeared condescending to staff and inmate-patients alike. Rumor was that his wife was also emotionally disturbed and a concert musician. No one ever saw her, and Dr. Van Yoder was very asocial as well.

"Some observers might say that there was sometimes difficulty in differentiating between inmate-patients and some healthcare staff, were it not for the standard color for prison attire. Dr. Van Yoder could be a very strange character with some odd behaviors. For example, he used to come to his office in the prison in the middle of the night, allegedly to catch up on reports and to correct all the alleged mistakes that he claimed were made by the secretaries. During a routine, random search of the mental health unit, COs found some very fancy female undergarments, including a leopard-skin bra and matching panties, in the doctor's office. Corrections staff also discovered a stash of reefer and a huge jar filled with amphetamines in his office! He never claimed his innocence or denied his sexual, cross-dressing fetish. However, he tacitly accepted responsibility for his substance abuse. He was not very forthcoming about his egregious disregard for prison rules and regulations.

"Previous to that, the COs cut Dr. Van Yoder some slack when he came to the mental-health unit in the middle of the night, hiding a two-foot long, steel, vacuum-cleaner pipe under his raincoat. The doctor proceeded to a psychotic inmate-patient's cell, woke up the patient, Julio Ortega, and began beating on the inmate's bed frame with the pipe, while chastising the inmate for calling him—the doctor—a faggot all the time! Sometimes even psychotic inmate-patients are very perceptive. But when all the contraband was found in Dr. Van Yoder's office, he was locked out of the prison indefinitely. He subsequently had a psychotic breakdown and, on one occasion, called mental-health staff at the mental-health unit, and was talking like an eight-year-old child, crying while also saying, 'Freud was a good man who loved children,' repeating this message several times. Days later, he sent me a page from a German gynecology textbook, the meaning of which has continued to escape me and the mental-health staff. Eventually, I called on the alcoholic chief psychiatrist, Dr. Mulrooney, to put Dr. Van Yoder away in a psychiatric treatment setting for a while because I was afraid that Dr. Van Yoder might harm himself.

"After psychiatric hospitalization and stabilization, Dr. Van Yoder was hidden away in a safe, non-threatening position at another security-treatment hospital where he was able to function indefinitely in his professional capacity. The mental-health team seriously doubted that there was any meaningful, in-depth treatment that would effectively address Dr. Van Yoder's several forms of madness, especially because of the doctor's arrogance and condescension.

"In Dr. Van Yoder's defense, what is amazing is that this doctor was also an astute diagnostician who really knew psychiatry and medicine. I'll never forget the time he admonished me for touting the value of education to a young inmate-patient, as though the academic pursuit was the most important goal in the young sociopath's life.

Dr. Van Yoder's words were, 'Don't you realize that an educated sociopath is even more dangerous in the absence of simultaneous moral development for the habitually, criminally-oriented felons!'

I understand now that he was absolutely correct."

Doctor Barilla continued: "Another interesting psychiatrist colleague was Dr. Simon Vukovich. His father was a youngster in an obscure Ukranian village who migrated to the ghettos of Warsaw, where he became a gifted tailor. Simon's dad, with other family members, then migrated to America in the mid-1930s, passing through the pearly gates of Ellis Island,to finally settle in the Flatbush section of Brooklyn, where Dr. Vukovich was born and raised.

"As an adult, he elevated the immigrant lessons of frugality to a new level, developing some manner of obsession and greed regarding monetary gain. Dr. Vukovich worked many part-time jobs as a psychiatrist, outside his full-time job as a state psychiatrist, and he was a major in the army reserves. He wore baggy, unkempt clothing to work and often had a malodorous scent about him. He walked with a boisterous swagger, his chin up in the air, with his lips pursed tightly and slightly puffed out, with a look of defiance and disdain, as if to say (and he did out loud at times), 'I don't give a damn about you mutts in here!' He drank COs' coffee and read their newspapers, and he had a crude, insensitive manner when dealing with inmate-patients. He was overheard in several interviews asking first, how much money they had in their account. His indelicate probing of their sexuality in confinement frequently began with the question, 'Do you suck cock?'

"Dr. Vukovich was frequently mocked by inmate-patients as he made daily rounds in the security-hospital wards. They would repeatedly chant in unison, 'Here comes the janitor!' When Dr. Vukovich reached the end of the psych ward, he would look back and emphatically flip off the inmate-patients, hollering out 'Fuck you,' and then quickly exit the unit. He was once observed in a surprising tirade, in the doctors' break room, while reading an article about actress Lucille Ball being a very wealthy woman. Apparently, Dr. Vukovich was envious that some female, nonmedical professional should be much wealthier than he? He was twice imprisoned for Medicaid fraud but managed to have his license reinstated. Like Dr. Van Yoder, he was properly licensed and was very knowledgeable in psychiatry and general medicine. Again, his bizarre personality precluded the possibility of providing empathic, effective, mental-health care in a maximum-security facility or anywhere else for that matter.

"These two psychiatrists were perfect examples of individuals with a high IQ and who were deficient in emotional intelligence. For example, they exhibited deficiencies in the area of self-awareness, self-control, empathy, social expertness, and personal influence. Repeated research on emotional intelligence has delivered a counter-intuitive finding that only one in four valedictorians make it to a high level of success in life."

*****

Then, after these and many other experiences in different units, working with staff that came and went, Dr. Barilla graduated to the maximum-security prison full time. In 1977, about three years after he started his career in state-government service, the state began to have a full-fledged psychiatric unit with inpatients/outpatient/daycare programming in all the maximum-security prisons. Doc B., as he was often called, also worked part-time over the years as an adjunct college instructor in psychology. He never stopped loving the teacher's role in his position as forensic psychologist, then as forensic-unit chief. He truly loved to learn, teach, share and explain ideas, theories, and practical applications in the treatment and management of inmates and inmate-patients in the unique culture of maximum-security prison.

Chapter 5

The Big House:
Maximum Security—the Last Stop

Once a person has made a choice that lands him in prison for a felony crime, the only option following the classification and reception process, which determines where an inmate should be placed as a prisoner (i.e. attitude, behavior, level of violence), is the minimum, medium, or maximum-security facility. Inmates know that there's no place left to go once they have reached that final stage in prison, namely, maximum security. It is now up to the inmate and everyone involved—the correctional staff, the medical staff, the administration, and even the inmate trustees—to strive to make this work on the inmate's behalf.

In his own words, here are Dr. Barilla's initial impressions when entering correctional service for the first time in a maximum-security prison.

"Unlike the earliest experience in the hospital for the criminally insane, which was eerie, strange, and seemingly unpredictable, the entry into the maximum-security prison exploded on all the senses. Once past the awe-inspiring thirty-foot cement wall with twelve gun towers surrounding the forty-five-acre prison setting, and once past the security screening through the front entrance, one got the impression of a multifaceted, busy movement of correctional personnel and inmates energetically attending to their personal business. The odors in the air were not always pleasant, especially on hot summer days. Loud, metallic, clanking noises abounded as COs with large metal skeleton keys, were constantly locking and unlocking huge, sliding, steel doors with metal bars on them. Over time, especially after the Attica riots in 1971, prisons installed more numerous checkpoints into the belly of the facility, which were either physically opened by COs or electronically controlled. And then, finally, I took the most wobbly elevator known to man to the second floor to the psychiatric satellite unit."

It would gradually become a more comfortable daily routine for Dr. Barilla to take the long walk from the front gate to the mental-health unit, exchanging amenities with uniformed and civilian staff, and inmates along the way.

"Morning, Lieutenant Burns. How's life in the knit shop with a few of our inmate patients on medication?"

The lieutenant was kind enough to give a few stable, chronic patients a chance to do part-time work in the shop on a trial basis.

"Fine for the most part, Doc. I'll keep an eye on Murphy. He's the most at risk for relapse."

The doctor was appreciative.

"Thanks for your cooperation and patience, Lieutenant."

Inmate Biaggio hollered to the doctor, "Thanks for helping my homeboy, Scott, with his depression. He's doing much better down on the cellblock."

"My pleasure," the doctor replied, suspecting the comment was less than honest, given the superficiality of the inmate who was always sucking up in some way.

Each day, as Dr. Barilla became more familiar with the interior areas of the prison, he, likewise, became more comfortable with the commands from the COs as their elevated voices, above the usual sounds of the prison, rang out. A few examples, which seemed self-explanatory, such as "On the visit," "On the school," "On the clinic," "On the library," or, "On the count," called the inmates to mandated or voluntary activities.

Dr. Barilla would finally arrive at the mental-health unit and get a report from the graveyard shift.

"Quiet night, Doc. Lucas wants the nurse to check his psych meds as soon as possible."

"Thanks, I'll pass it on right away, Harry. Good looking out, as usual."

Harry Lewis was a long-time, reliable CO on the midnight shift. Soon after, the full, daytime mental-health team would arrive, discuss issues/

strategies for the day, and proceed to do therapy, dispense medications, and handle any needed crisis interventions. The crucial hand-off information, from shift to shift in the mental-health unit, was very professional, using the SBAR method, meaning addressing problems with attention to Situation, Background, Assessment, and Recommendation to incoming staff. Among key staff members were chief psychiatrist Charles Lee, head nurse Mark Lopez, lead CO Heinrich Sherbach, and unit operations manager Noel Baratta. These employees, along with others, such as the mental health staff who ran the unit for chronically mentally ill inmate-patients, made Dr. Barilla's job as unit chief much easier, as they provided a high level of security and facilitated the quality mental-health services throughout the prison. CO Sherbach was sharp, disciplined, organized, and a good leader of his uniformed staff. Nurse Lopez was wise, patient, and a wonderful, empathetic handler of even the most difficult inmate-patients. Dr. Lee and social worker Herb Franklin were empathic and skillful at treating our most vulnerable, chronically ill inmate-patients. Ms. Baratta was tough, competent, and extremely efficient in facilitating the general mental-health operations. Her tough reputation was once strengthened when she felt compelled to verbally demean a sociopathic inmate who loudly asked her, "Hey, Noel, are you still fuckin' Dr. Barilla?"

Noel walked up close to the screened opening of the inmate's observation cell and responded, "Listen, you piece of shit! Take care of your own fucked-up business and maybe your sorry punk ass will have a chance to survive your sentence in prison."

Noel then emphatically flipped off the locked-up inmate and walked back to her office in a secure area.

*****

Every three to four months, the prison authorities mandated orientation for new employees in the prison. The half-day program offered the general information about physical structure, programs, staffing, prison history, and repeated emphasis on security and potential dangers in the challenging environment of a maximum-security prison. The incredible display of inmate-manufactured weapons, usually made out of "raw materials" almost always fascinated new employees. The last part of the program was opened up to questions from new employees, with various uniformed and civilian leaders, including Dr. Barilla, offering answers and explanations. Oftentimes, the warden, Mr. Mulligan, would participate and offer his perspective on the culture of maximum-security prisons.

Dr. Barilla was impressed by the huge repertoire of confiscated homemade weapons on display during orientation. In addition to the resourcefulness of inmates making dangerous devices out of seemingly innocuous material, there was a clear indication of creative cruelty in the mix. For example, there was the toothbrush with razor blades attached to both sides. The intention of this weapon was to maim the victim, especially in the facial area, with deep wounds that would be difficult to suture and probably leave scars for a lifetime! Research showed that cutting or piercing weapons were mostly used on inmate attacks of othe᠎ inmates, while blunt objects were more often used in inmate attacks on staff.

Many new employees at orientation asked questions about religious issues in prison.

"Deputy Corrigan, what are the percentages of various religions in the prison?"

Deputy Corrigan responded, "Research data consistently reveal that United States prisons have about 40 percent Roman Catholics, 35 percent Protestants, about 7 percent Muslims, about 3 percent Native Americans, and a very small percentage of all other religions. Typically, there are very few management problems with the two major religions in prison. Despite much smaller numbers, Muslims have been politically active in our prison and often are investigated for illegal activities. For example, a former chief Muslim chaplain of the New York State Department of Corrections, who influenced many other Muslim chaplains and inmate Muslims in New York and many other state prisons, was quoted once as saying: 'The Koran does not forbid terrorism even against the innocent. This is the sort of teaching they don't want in prison, but this is what I'm doing.' Terrorism within the homeland USA has been fomented by radical Muslim offshoots, such as the five-percenters and wahabism, which are very transparent with their philosophy of hate and violence!"

Agnes Wittiker, a new social worker in the mental-health unit, asked, "What about other religious groups that pose problems in prison?"

Father Riley, a long-time Catholic Chaplain, replied, "Although we don't see it much here, white-supremacist groups like the World Church of the Creator and the corrupted Asatru religion, use the cover of religion to hide illegal activities in prison and to hide the underlying philosophy of hate and violence. Some states, like Kentucky, have outlawed satanic services in prison. Massachusetts has made allowances for Native Americans to utilize authentic purification lodges among their services to minority religious groups. Most states now scrutinize any religious groups and practices that promote or have a history of violence and intolerance of legally protected groups."

Bill Hebert, a new corrections counselor, asked: "Is religion viewed by inmates and correctional staff as a valuable part of rehabilitation?"

Warden Mulligan replied, "By all means. Hopefully, the majority of inmates involved in religious practices in prison do embrace and benefit from involvement in religious beliefs and principles. The problem is we don't always know who is sincere, and the old trick of Bible-totin' inmates appearing before the parole board has created lots of skepticism over the years. The other reality is that the acid test for religiously founded, principled living, won't be seriously tested until the inmate returns to the free community."

Father Riley jumped in, "By the way, atheists or agnostics have seldom been viewed as problem inmates solely because of their religious preference. This correctional facility makes every reasonable effort to accommodate religious practice and tolerance for the small minority religious groups such as Hindu, Mormon, or Jehovah's Witness. The troublesome white supremacist group, Aryan Brotherhood, who make up less than one-tenth of one percent of the nation's prison population, are reported by the FBI to be responsible for 18 percent of all prison murders!"

CO rookie, Fred Tippen, asked the deputy of security, Mr. Cooper, "What are some common homemade weapons and can their use be prevented in some way?"

Deputy Cooper answered, "Many homemade weapons are made from medically prescribed items like knee braces, canes, and crutches and from general prison-store items like toothbrushes, padlocks, and razors, and from workplace items such as metal and wooden poles, strips of metal, and kitchen implements, such as forks, spoons, and so on."

CO Tippen impatiently blurted, "Can you *ever* prevent the risk of violence with all of this?"

Deputy Cooper responded, "Besides the snitch or informant network, which we often use to our advantage, we've learned some other clever strategies over time. One of the best is to leak a wire—that's a message that spreads rapidly—that a whole cellblock of 250 inmates will be searched tomorrow morning without warning. Through the night, one can hear clanking noises on each of the six company floors as inmates shed their secret stash of weapons to avoid serious disciplinary consequences. Literally, dump trucks have been used to remove the huge confiscation of illegal weapons, and,as inmates know, a good percentage of individual cells are still randomly searched to ensure complete removal of homemade weapons on the cellblock in question."

Warden Mulligan wrapped up the orientation by urging all new employees, civilian and uniformed, to "closely observe the rules and call upon seasoned employees for answers to questions, dilemmas, and inmate requests."

Mr. Mulligan tactfully informed the group about past examples of irresponsible employee behaviors that resulted in dismissal and/or criminal charges.

*****

Having reached this point, Dr. Barilla began to experience numerous other incidents that helped to develop his background and are important to view when considering how he became very qualified as a clinical psychologist in a setting where such expertise is desperately needed. Most licensed, trained psychologists would opt out of prison work in favor of more lucrative and safer positions in the private realm. Clinical treatment has a few similarities in both the maximum-security prison and in private practice in the free community, but there are many more critical differences, which clinicians must constantly be aware of at all times in the unique prison setting.

Dr. Barilla really enjoyed sharing his unusual, interesting clinical experiences with all corrections and mental-health staff, especially newcomers in the prison culture.

At the Thursday morning think-tank meeting, new assistant programs director, Victor Jordan, said: "Doc B., tell us about some of your memorable challenges."

The doctor had many stories.

"At one point, there was an inmate-patient, Daryl Spencer, who used to call himself 'Frequency Modulation.' This inmate-patient would always wrap one of the lenses in his eyeglasses with aluminum foil. He would also fashion a tiny aluminum antenna and place that on the frame of the glasses where it meets the lens. He claimed he was getting all kinds of messages from somewhere in outer space, and as a result, he had a preoccupation with starting a sperm bank to which he would be the major contributor. Daryl would carry around with him pictures from what was called in prison 'short heist' magazines, which were really nothing but pornography. He would cut out photos of women's vaginas, and he would pull out this little stack of pictures and show them to everyone he met, saying that he had 'pussy power.' That was his expression. Because of his connection to the ethereal, he christened himself Frequency Modulation. With his compliance with psychiatric medications and therapy, he would stabilize for a while and be less preoccupied with vaginas and pussy power."

Psychiatrist, Dr. Woo, asked if there have been many inmate-patients with past military experience.

Doc B. continued, "There had been an inmate-patient, a very interesting person, Harry Harrison, who was actually honorably discharged from the army. He had numerous jobs in his lifetime but got himself into trouble with drugs and a robbery charge that was lost in plea bargaining. Harry would intermittently have problems with periods of psychosis, which would require treatment and medication, although he spent quite a bit of time in the general population doing his relatively brief sentence in a reasonably productive manner. There was no known trauma during his military service, and there were no symptoms of Post Traumatic Stress Disorder. Once, while in a psychotic state, Harry asked to go see the superintendent of the prison (still known as the warden) with a request. Since Harry had no wife and no family and the prison allowed for conjugal visits for inmates who kept their behavior in order, Harry wanted to ask the warden if he could have conjugal visits with a blow-up doll. Now, I thought that was pretty creative, and I considered that if I was on that committee that granted requests for intimate visits, I might have given that some thought and possibly let Harry go out there in that trailer, reserved for such visits, with his blow-up doll and be able to do his thing for the allowed thirty hours.

"There were also occasions when Harry spent time in the mental-health inpatient unit standing at parade rest, with his feet spread apart and his hands clasped behind his back, and he would say that he was on alert for sex offenders. They would be either 'rapos'—inmates who raped people their own age—or the ones that were most despised, even more than rapos, the ones who were called 'baby-fuckers'—the child molesters—especially those who had done it over an extended period of time. Harry claimed, standing in front of the nurses' station on our mental-health unit, that he could spot the inmates who were sex offenders. What was truly uncanny is that most of the time, he was right! And some of the other patients coming up for medication or to ask questions would be kind of leery being around Harry. The staff, of course, had to keep their eye on him as well.

"There was another occasion that was interesting and involved Harry. It was a time when he was in the Box. He had gotten himself into trouble by getting into a fight and then giving a corrections officer a hard time. They locked him up in the Disciplinary Special Housing Unit, called the Box. So the entire mental-health crew—one of the psychiatrists, the head nurse, the unit chief, and myself (at the time I was the psychologist on staff and not yet the unit chief)—went up to see Harry in the Box. He was usually interesting to talk to, usually reasonably polite, and usually reasonably coherent.

"However, when we arrived there, Harry had a very somber look on his face as he walked right up to the cell door, and he began to go down the line and point his finger at each one of the staff in an accusatory manner.

"He looked at me, knowing that I was Italian-American, and he said, 'You, dago Mafia! You sell drugs to my people!'

"Then, he looked at Victor Krause, who was actually German-American, but Harry thought he was Jewish, and he said to Victor, 'You, Kike Jew bastard! You screw my people in the community in your stores and everything!'

"Then, he looked at Betty Simmons, the head nurse, who was a white woman, and he said, 'You, white lady! You like our *big* black boys, don't you?'

"And then this little, timid, kind, consulting Japanese psychiatrist, Dr. Matzuzaka, was standing there petrified, and Harry pointed at him and said, 'You! Jap! You bombed Pearl Harbor! You attacked our country. You lousy fuckin' rat!'

"The staff all decided at that point that Harry just did his own ethnic cleansing thing, and they better get out of that situation for now and come back to see Harry at a better time, when he was stabilized with his medication and generally more agreeable. He was definitely an interesting character."

*****

The new corrections captain, Richard Shipley, asked: "Doc, do you ever have to go down into the cellblocks to do crisis intervention or treatment of any kind?"

Doc B. recounted a suicidal crisis he had addressed.

"I went to a cellblock where a Hispanic inmate had his cell door jammed shut with a little end table. He was holding a razor to his throat. He was bleeding both from his throat and from his hands, and he had written on the wall with his own blood that he wanted to die. The exact words in Spanish were: ¡*Me quiero morir! ¡Me quiero matar!*' I was eventually able to convince him to come out of the cell, to put the razor down, and to come with me up to the mental-health unit for evaluation and possible admission. But when a staff member goes down to a cellblock in a situation like that, everybody has to lock in—all the tiers and all the companies—until the crisis is resolved, and man, do those inmates hate that. On that occasion, they were all screaming from their cells, 'Cut your throat you motherfucker! I wanna go to the yard! I wanna go to my class, you son-of-a-bitch! Cut your throat and die!' Many expressions like those were spewed out by the angry inmates in that cellblock. Meanwhile, the staff were trying to do sensitive crisis intervention in the midst of all that screaming and it is not always easy."

Doc B. related another situation with risk for self-harm.

"Then there was an inmate-patient, a big husky guy, who used to draw pictures of penises in his cell. His fetish was discovered by other inmates who then teased him mercilessly about his drawings and questioned him about his gender preference. The inmate-patient became very frightened one day from their mockery and he was at the end of his wits. As they say on the street, 'All that stuff got on his last nerve.' The inmate-patient climbed up the screens to the third tier and was threatening to jump off. Just as in the previous example, the inmates then began shouting, 'Jump, motherfucker! I wanna get outta here! I don't wanna see this crap! Go ahead! Kill yourself!' There was a common lack of sympathy and empathy among incarcerated felons.

"Somehow, the staff managed to get the inmate-patient to come down from the screening and they brought him up to the psychiatric unit, put him on inpatient status briefly, medicated him, and ultimately sent him to the security-treatment hospital for more intensive inpatient psychiatric care. Just previous to this inmate-patient's admission to the inpatient psychiatric hospitalization, he refused the admission in a violent manner and had to be physically and chemically restrained before transfer to the security-treatment inpatient hospital."

*****

Doc B. explained some recent history in corrections.

"Previously, there had been two hospitals for the criminally insane, one was in the southern part of the state, and the other was way up near the New Hampshire border. In time, they revised the system, one of those ever-evolving positive things, and eliminated the two hospitals in favor of one centrally-located prison psychiatric center. In fact, that is what it is now called: the Martinsville Security Psychiatric Center. It is situated in the center of the state. In the prison setting, whenever anyone gets two PC's (two physician certificates), wherein two physicians—one has to be a psychiatrist—sign a petition to have an inmate-patient hospitalized in an emergency situation, this begins a specialized process. Originally, this was a ten-step method, which took up to two weeks, because it involved doctors, lawyers, judges, mental-health advisors, along with security-hospital bed availability, before a decision could be rendered that allowed this transfer to take place. Because it took so long, the process was finally changed to allow an immediate transfer based upon the recommendation of the psychiatrist and another physician. This ten-step process is now completed after the emergency transfer of an inmate-patient to the security hospital. And that is where they send all violent, psychotically-disturbed individuals."

Some staff had heard about the "cocktail" and questioned Doc B. about what they thought was illegal manufacture of booze.

Doc volunteered, "Let me explain the history of the problem and the solution. One of the most challenging situations, and maybe one of the most creative interventions I have done in my career in that setting, was during one of the epidemics that came about every once in a while in which inmates, especially those in the Box, but sometimes in general population, would mix what I affectionately called a 'cocktail.' Inmates would take urine, semen, and feces, and mix it all up in a cup—sometimes with the addition of spit—and, if they did not like a staff person, especially a civilian, they would throw the cocktail at that person.

"The cocktail throwers were a little bit leery about doing it to a correction officer for fear of reprisal. However, those inmates in the Box might do it to the COs as well because the inmates there were locked up for a year or two or three or more, or they might already be doing a life sentence. Therefore, they often figured they had nothing to lose. As a result, someone in corrections got the bright idea of putting a plastic shield over the cell door of any cocktail thrower. The problem with that was that there would have to be a 'feed-up hatch' installed in the middle of the plastic shield on the door, in order to give the inmates their meals. The inmates who liked to throw cocktails around would now throw the cocktails through the plastic feed-up hatch in the middle of the door! They got real good at it! Then somebody got another bright idea of putting the feed-up hatch at the lower end of the plastic shield near the bottom of the cell door. Well, of course, the resourceful inmates, locked up in that situation, found a way to accurately throw the cocktail contents on somebody, even from the lower feed-up hatch. Back in the day, if any inmate did anything like that, the COs would go in there with hoses and nightsticks and kick butts and take names, hose the inmates down, and beat them up, which would usually solve the problem for a while. But it did not mean the barbaric behavior would stop.

"Anyway, I came up with an idea after the security staff, along with the deputy superintendent of security, asked me for some help with this problem. I knew the reason they asked was because, in the past, there had been no effective support or remedy for this degenerate behavior forthcoming from the corrections headquarters in the state capitol. Additionally, the frightening issues surrounding the advent of AIDS, provided justification, in my mind, to make this dreadful misconduct a mental-health issue. The initial, official word was that we were afraid that the AIDS virus was in urine, and in spit, and the state had only a limited budget to utilize for an answer to this problem.

"As we worked together well with the administration, we bought metal gloves out of our mental health budget that looked like what the knights might have worn in medieval times in the jousting matches. We ordered these for the correctional staff in the Box because we knew that the corrections officers would be afraid of being bitten and spit upon by the inmates they had to handle. We also knew that this would continue to build the collaboration we've enjoyed with the administration and how we eagerly help each other in times of need.

"The security leaders called me up and, with much anxiety, said, 'Doc B., can you help us? The administration in the capitol said they cannot do much about it, and we're just going to have to deal with these mutts throwing this cocktail in the best way that we can.'

"I responded by saying, 'You know, let me think about this and I'll get back to you within a day.'

"We figured the best way to work through this problem was to treat it as though it was a psychiatric anomaly, and I devised a plan. The minute we got word in the psychiatric unit that there was a threat that resulted in a cocktail being thrown, the plan was that corrections staff would initiate certain actions.

Mental-health staff would go up to the Box with the psychiatrist and the Box sergeant in tow, and they would address the perpetrator: 'Mr. Smith, we think something is wrong with your mind. We're going to bring you down to the Psychiatric Unit on the second floor of the prison, and put you under a psychiatric observation and evaluation to make sure that you are okay.'

"And that is what we would do in the event of a cocktail being thrown at *any* staff in the prison. The corrections staff would take the perpetrator down to the Psychiatric Unit, on the second floor, and remove all of their clothing and personal possessions, and then put the inmate-patient in a paper gown and underwear, and then place them on an observation watch in a psychiatric-observation cell. The inmate-patient in that status would get their meals on Styrofoam trays, and they would be required to scoop their food with Styrofoam cups because no utensils or any kind of sharp or metal objects were allowed during that twenty-four-hour watch period. There would be no smoking, no coffee, no privileges, and no typical clothing for twenty-four hours.

"This procedure was phenomenally successful, because one of the things that inmates do not want to happen to them, these big tough guys, is they don't want to be disempowered.

"Furthermore, the inmate-patient was told in that situation, 'If you try to plug up your toilet or act out in any violent way, we're going to come into the observation cell and stick a needle in your ass and put you to sleep. We will do this procedure as long as you continue to act out. Be cool and you think about what you did, how barbaric that behavior was with the throwing the cocktail at staff, and how dangerous it is to yourself and to other inmates in terms of hygiene and safety. For example, your feces and semen and urine might contain the AIDS virus. If you stay in control for the twenty-four-hour observation period, we'll give you back your privileges and send you back to the housing area from which you came.'

"Typically, after twenty-four hours in that situation, if they did well and were compliant, the staff would give them back their clothes and would send them back to their cellblock with restored privileges.

"Staff would also tell them, 'Look, if you are frustrated or you got a problem, we'll come up and see you. We'll talk to you. We'll help you. And when you get out of the Box and are in general population again, we will have you come up to mental health as an outpatient for appointments to receive counseling. We'll do everything we can for you within the limits of the correctional setting. But *do not* engage in that dangerous, barbaric behavior or you will be back in this situation again!'

"Once more, vicarious learning can be powerful. We never saw a man come back a second time with the need to be placed in this observation situation, and when the wire quickly spread as to how these cocktail throwers were handled in the mental-health observation unit, the 'epidemic' came to a screeching halt!"

Sgt. Pierce, a new corrections supervisor in the mental health unit, asked Doc B., "Did the COs in the Box receive any special training for the strategy you described with the shit-throwers? And did you need to get approval from your supervisors in mental health?"

"Important questions, Sarge," Doc B. responded. "I'll first tell you that my staff supported the plan 100 percent, but we did trial runs without seeking permission from HQ in the capitol. They were too busy up there doing CYA, sweatin' about lawsuits, liberal inmate advocacy groups, prisoners' legal services, and general inertia, ad nauseam. We needed to take decisive actions ASAP.

"My training with the Box correctional staff, including leadership, was brief, intensive, thorough, and was permeated with the following message: 'Men, here's the deal with our involvement to eliminate the shit-throwing episodes in the Box. My team and I are excited about working with you guys, and we know how tough it is up here. In order to justify our work with you, we have to follow certain guidelines and we absolutely need your cooperation or we'll all be in more serious shit than the stuff flyin' around here. We will respond to your call *immediately* to take away any inmate who throws the *cocktail*, that is, any combination of feces, urine, semen or saliva, *not water*!

"Please do not antagonize or challenge any inmate to do this behavior. It must be something they decide to do on their own, and only under that condition can we justify putting them in a strip-cell for twenty-four-hours observation down in our mental-health unit. If we are satisfied that they are stable at the end of twenty-four hours in observation and if they convince us that this barbaric behavior will not be repeated, we'll return them to resume their time in the Box. We may decide to add them to our list of Box inmate-patients whom we visit on regular rounds in Special Housing Unit.

"If we work closely together on this, I'm quite certain this nasty nonsense will stop shortly. When an inmate returns to the Box from observation with us, I guarantee you that a wire will go all through SHU that 'these crazy motha-fuckas don't play, man! Step off with that throwin' stuff cuz you'll be in paper panties in a motha-fuckin empty cell with *no privileges*, and some pervert CO eye-ballin' your ass the whole time! And if you break off on them, they'll stick a needle in your ass and put you out for the count!' That kind of wire can stop a lot of stupid, nasty behavior in a hurry. The inhibiting impact of this whole procedure, on other would-be perpetrators of cocktail-throwing, is called *vicarious learning* in behavioral psychology.' I always added at the end of training sessions, 'The deal is on; good luck everybody!' "

*****

Ms. Wittaker asked Doc B., "Any unique or serious problems with blatant, aggressive homosexual behavior?"

Doc always enjoyed relating this story: "On a lighter note, we had an inmate who was a very interesting individual.

"One day, mental health got a call from the Box sergeant who said, 'Doc B., you gotta come up to the Box and see this guy, Pedro Quirjuan. He's got bigger tits than Marilyn Monroe. Oh, my God, you've got to come up here!' So I went up to the Box and talked to this inmate. I could not believe his name, Quirjuan, pronounced 'queer-one,' a perfect fit. He was a Hispanic homosexual man. Before his incarceration, he had found this doctor in the free community who indiscriminately gave people like him hormone treatments so that they could build up their hips and their breasts.

"However Pedro had no desire to give up his genitals; he liked his male genitals. As a homosexual he enjoyed the sexual experience of climaxing, and he wanted to have sexual encounters with men. He wanted to make himself attractive to men. Well, one can only imagine how, in an all-male maximum-security prison, a man with a figure like this, strutting around and flashing himself can only create all kinds of behavior problems. Pedro would sashay around his cellblock and, when the administration finally let him out of the Box and put him in general population again, he would sashay around in a long, red, silk-like robe, swishing all over the place and getting all kinds of attention. And here are these inmates on the cellblock, drooling and fighting about who was going to have this attractive homosexual inmate as their 'kid,' the name given to an inmate who does one's sexual bidding. Like a play toy, it is his kid.

"All these inmates were dreaming about going down the 'Hershey Highway,' as they say in prison, or going down the 'Dirt Road,' and couldn't wait to bend this guy over and 'pack his fudge!'

"But what this Quirjuan did was fight with a lot of people and tried to make his own decision about which inmates he would have a relationship with. He would be what might be called a 'fightin' fag.' At one time, he stabbed another inmate very badly and corrections finally sent him to another prison, which was really beneficial for everybody else involved, because this kind of character can create a great deal of chaos in a cellblock, in fact, the whole prison. Quirjuan was an interesting person to talk to, though. He wasn't psychotic. He wasn't looking for a transgender change, where he was going to become a woman. He was just a blatant homosexual who pulled out all the stops and did everything he could to attract men to him to have homosexual affairs. It truly made for a very troublesome experience that had everybody scratching their head."

"Wow, what a character!" exclaimed Ms. Wittaker. "Is it true that every inmate has to belong to a group of some kind to survive in prison?"

Doc said, "It's usually true, but there are some unique exceptions. There were a few inmates during my career who were called the Moby Dicks of prison because these individuals were all big men who were powerful, dangerous, and feared by virtually all other inmates. They didn't pump iron, and they didn't hang out with the boys on what is called the Spot, where inmates work out, doing exercises and do body building. Instead, these guys kept to themselves, each one with his own modus operandi, just doing his own thing. One Haitian guy, Pierre Fortier, who had only one good eye left from his violent life, just wanted to be left alone as much as possible and actually stayed in his cell as much as possible. Another, Bo Richards, just wanted to clean all the time—give him a bucket of water with soap and he was content. And another, Vince Fortuna, had the power and a fist that could pound a person's head into mush. He didn't like being locked in a cell all the time. Corrections officers sometimes would actually let him sleep outside his cell because they really thought he had the power to bend the bars on the cell door and break his way out. And then there was one inmate, Jason Lackey, who just liked to eat a lot, so correction officers made sure that he was well fed.

"One of these Moby Dick types, Paulie Bruno, was a sinewy hulk who was extremely powerful, very strong, very clever, and who liked to find drugs, get high, and 'sell tickets.' What is meant by that is, an inmate is threatening another inmate in the cell next to him. If one inmate 'cashes in' a ticket, that means the offended inmate is going to meet the threatening inmate outside their cells or out in the yard and fight it out. When the correction officers would go to subdue Paulie, to bring him up to the psychiatric unit when he was acting crazy, Paulie would find some baby oil and grease himself up, so the officers couldn't hold him down and couldn't tackle him without serious difficulty. It would be one long, drawn-out battle to get Paulie secured, subdued, and restrained in order to bring him up to the psychiatric unit.

"After one such violent, chaotic episode, Sergeant Breen said to me., 'Having fun yet, Doc?'

"I responded, 'Good jail, good jail!'

"This was a popular expression used by COs and civilian staff when rough situations were resolved. It was a form of machismo, false bravado, seeming to offer some reassurance that this difficult work was manageable, maybe even enjoyable."

Nurse Barron asked Doc B., "Aside from hanging, which is the most common method of suicide in prison; are there other kinds of self-destructive behaviors you've encountered?"

Doc responded enthusiastically: "On occasion we have had other peculiar incidents like the inmate-patient, Junior Smalls, who was frustrated and was on a suicide watch. He would bang his head into the metal cell door and charge all the way across the cell while driving his head into the feed-up hatch, doing that several times before staff could get in and stop him. When we cleaned up the door opening around the feed-up hatch, we removed large pieces of his scalp and hair, and we had to sedate him and then send him off to the security-treatment hospital

"This was similar in scope to another inmate who was a young adult in psychiatric care and had been found incompetent to stand trial because of his mental instability. He was released back to jail but did not want to go. To get out of this situation, he pounded his head onto a sharp pencil, accurately aiming at one eye. The pencil penetrated his skull through his eye. He lived and eventually went back to trial, blind in one eye. One other example of this type of self-harm was with an inmate-patient who was on suicide watch who tried to pull his eye out. He had a long history of psychotic episodes, bizarre behavior, issues with his homosexuality, including an attempt to get a sex change while serving his sentence, and lots of guilt associated with the brutal murder he committed that brought him to prison.

"His family background included a history of multiple drug abuses, a mother who was an alcoholic, and a very violent, abusive father whose actions resulted in a great deal of domestic abuse during this inmate-patient's youth and during his developmental years in general. Using the stem of a plastic spoon, he attempted to pry his eye out, reportedly in an effort to keep his mind from seeing all the things that he had witnessed, both willingly and unwillingly, from his distressing early years. All three of these cases reflect extremely rare forms of deliberate self-harm, the last one called self-enucleation.

"In my experiences, while conducting my earlier private practice, I encountered one other very unusual case of a woman named Kim Ling, a twenty-two-year old, who was diagnosed with schizophrenia and had been admitted to a psychiatric ward on several occasions. What motivated her to acts of self-destruction were reported auditory hallucinations that commanded her to injure herself. When the voices spoke, they were very offensive and insulting, according to the patient. In her last episode, the voices were so loud that she could not hear the staff at the hospital speaking to her.

"She was treated with antipsychotic medication and electroconvulsive therapy, but these interventions did not diminish the episodes. Following one particularly strong increase in her medication, including physical as well as chemical restraints, she was overly distressed by her hallucinations. Somehow, she managed to damage her left eye to the degree that her vision was irreparably lost. When interviewed later, Kim Ling said that her act of self-harm was a response to her command hallucinations.

"She said, 'God instructed me to gouge out my eye.'

"It is interesting to note that after this last episode, Kim Ling's mental state improved and stabilized, and she was discharged from inpatient psychiatric treatment and even outpatient therapy, with only continuing mild medications as a form of treatment."

Doc continued, "Deliberate self-harm can be something that covers the spectrum of being mild, including picking of the skin and hair-pulling, to the more serious forms like self-cutting, genital mutilation, self-amputation, and self-enucleation. As can be seen by the former examples, these actions can be either from an intent to commit suicide, from mental delusion, or from an intention to manipulate the system for some personal gain."

*****

Doc was asked by Ms. Cooper, "Have you dealt with any infamous characters whose crimes and trials reached the level of wide-spread publicity, even before incarceration?"

"Absolutely!" Doc said. "On one occasion, there was an inmate, Darius Washington, a dangerous young man who at a very early age (preteen and teen) killed people on the subway for fun. And Centerville Correctional Facility had him in prison on an out-count (a temporary transfer of an inmate) from another penitentiary. Some of the prisons that did not have full-fledged psychiatric units or cou'd not deal with a certain troublesome inmate, could send that inmate to our unit for evaluation and stabilization. Darius had cleverly swallowed a handcuff key and would not give it back to the corrections officers. As a favor to the security deputy of the sending prison, I agreed to put Darius in a lockup, observation cell for a period of time. Darius furtively passed the key a couple of times in his feces. Somehow or another, he repeatedly recovered the key, cleaned it, and swallowed it again.

"Finally, at the end of about one week, we established a pretty good rapport with Darius and told him this observation cell procedure was not going to end until we got the key from him. Furthermore, if he was cool at the end, maybe we would give him a treat. Darius finally produced the key. It was on a Saturday. I came into work with a pizza for my staff, and we gave Darius a couple of pieces of pizza to reward his cooperation and then sent him back to the Box in his assigned prison. This successful procedure was actually a great example of 'Time-Out' in behavioral psychology. Darius had been doing time in the Box in his whole prison career, and he will remain in prison for life.

"At one time, while in another prison, Warren Correctional Facility, a newspaper reporter came to visit Darius to talk about his life as a young, notorious felon doing time. This resourceful inmate had managed to stash a knife somewhere in the visiting room, undetected by any of the correctional staff. For no apparent reason, Darius stood up on a table in the visiting room and began ranting about his proud, lifelong defiance, with this reporter sitting there (the reporter probably being someone very high on the misguided benevolence scale). Suddenly, this outrageous behavior struck the reporter who was shocked to see this sociopathic killer jump up on the table, while screaming obscenities. And when a correction officer came over to calm the situation down, Darius lashed out at the CO with the knife he had recovered from its hiding place. He stabbed the CO through and through. Fortunately, the officer lived but he was bleeding like a stuck pig. Finally, Darius was subdued by others, but the reporter was vomiting all over the place before fainting while sitting in his chair at the visiting room table. He had to be carried out and given some kind of first aid. This is a clear example of how unpredictable and dangerous Darius was, and these are some of the scenes in maximum-security prison that one might witness any time, any day.

"I also happened to be visiting Warren Correctional Facility that day and was called to the visiting room after the incident with Darius.

As often was the case, Sergeant Vizio, who was an excellent sergeant when at Centerville State Prison, orchestrated the cessation of the violent incident and asked me 'Doc, you okay?'

"I got some comfort in reciting the mantra, however cynical: good jail! good jail!"

The doctor continued to offer examples of notorious crimes:

"There was an inmate-patient, Leon Chomski, who I mentioned earlier, who was a long-term patient at Martinsville Security Treatment Hospital who had, like so many others, done some inpatient hospitalization, had done a lot of outpatient treatment, and a had lot of time on medication. This particular inmate-patient, among other things, wanted to have a sex change. Leon and his girlfriend, when he was a young man, had been taken in by a nurse when the couple had run away from home and had no place to go. One day, Leon and his girlfriend decided to kill this nurse and take her car and her possessions. They tied a rope around the nurse's neck leaving both ends extended several feet. Then they each took an end of the rope and went in opposite directions, pulling with all their might on the rope, strangling the poor women to death. The girl was sent to a women's prison and got out after a few years.

"Leon received a life sentence and just became more bizarre and more disturbed as time went on. It was during this period, that he announced he wanted to have a sex change. The psychiatric staff had to deal with this very unusual request. They told Leon how, in responsible clinics in the free community, it is a long process where one must cross-dress for a couple of years—not just as a transvestite and not as a homosexual. One had to really believe he was a woman in a man's body. First, he must try to live a normal life cross-dressing, and then have the electrolysis to remove his beard, while taking various hormones to increase his hips and breasts. Then, the very last thing is the removal of the male genitals and the implanting of the female genitals. Leon was politely told that all of that was not going to happen in prison. Leon was very distraught about not being able to do the transgender process.

"Leon endured a lot of persecution from inmate peers over the years. One time, he received a gift from the other inmates who were ridiculing him. He was always the target now for predators and homosexuals during his prison sentence. The inmates in question gave Leon a necklace made of razorblades and said to him, 'Here, pal, this is something that you can use that suits you properly.' Leon made many suicide attempts and, one time while on a suicide watch, he had his back to the door of his observation cell and kept walking away from the door, while keeping one hand up to his face. When he was asked by correctional staff to turn around and face the staff at the door, they noticed that one of his eyes was all red; he had actually been trying to remove his eyeball with his index finger! This is another example of self-enucleation, which is pretty rare, but does sometimes happen in inpatient psychiatric settings."

*****

Ms. Cooper brought up the subject of boundaries that need to be clearly identified.

"Doc B., have you seen many problems with staff becoming enmeshed with inmates?"

Doc shook his head with a concerned, even sad, look.

"Some staff. who didn't listen and learn about this crucial matter, met with tragic consequences! For example, there had been some female employees who, unfortunately, got involved with inmates in various ways. One staff member, Jennifer Barnett, was a recreational therapist, who was a bizarre person in her own right. She used to send pictures of her vagina to her boyfriend in the military in the demilitarized zone in Korea just to piss him off and to make him envy the fact that some other guy might be enjoying his old girlfriend now. Her message was, if he wanted to get any action with her, he better get his butt home. This female employee was caught performing fellatio in the bathroom in one of the treatment program areas for regular inmates. These were not the inmate-patients, the chronic inmate-patients who she was supposed to be providing treatment for, who received her unethical 'services.' Instead, they were some of the slick con men who would drift into the program area inappropriately, and she would service them!"

"Wow!" exclaimed a few of the staff.

"Unbelievable!" came another of the staff responses.

Dr. Barilla reminded everyone what the warden said to new employees about caution.

He continued: "We had a nurse, Emily Morse, who was more subtle and gradually got more and more involved with inmates. This, of course, detracted from her nursing duties. She began to take part in religious services, specifically Muslim. And then she began to get romantically connected to a lifer when she took a different job in the institution. She left nursing and went to work for the superintendent because the administration thought that Emily was someone with good skills who could relate well to the inmates. Some people, who had known her from the streets, asked the question of some of the staff who worked there, 'Is Emily up there fucking all the inmates yet, because she will in time?' No one knew that she had that kind of reputation or history in the free community. Emily ended up getting totally involved with this lifer, Joel Harris, and she had to quit her job. She ended up coming back as a civilian, and she married Joel, despite his life sentence. That is not uncommon, as the correctional staff has seen quite a bit of inappropriate romantic involvement with staff and inmates over the years. It is just too bad that this happened to be one of the facility's psychiatric nurses, and a pretty good nurse at that, just in terms of her nursing skills."

*****

Doc B. would sometimes invite mental-health lawyer, Sam Benson, to co-present programs to staff on important issues of legal responsibility, such as suicide and deliberate indifference.

Sam took the lead: "As you've heard before, suicide problems with some of the inmates is a very serious problem because, as time goes on, suicides present a very expensive proposition in addition to the unfortunate business of losing a life. It presents problems legally, as families have learned that inmate death by suicide can be moneymakers. Families of incarcerated suicidal victims become litigious and will gladly sue the state for large amounts of money if any 'deliberate neglect' is determined. That is the legal term for trying to discern whether or not personnel from the facility failed to do their job properly—deliberate indifference, deliberate neglect.

"All staff have to pay attention to this issue, and there has been a lot of training in the state system over the years, especially in the latter part of the twentieth century. Suicide prevention got to be a pretty effective approach, especially improvements in screening people and their tendencies. One of the dilemmas is that inmates and inmate-patients, who did a lot of self-harmful behavior, seldom succeeded in committing suicide. But they require a lot of attention and a lot of intervention. It's a case of the squeaky wheel getting the grease. The few completed suicides that happened were not really predictable, maybe with one exception. But the few that happened during Doc B.'s long correctional career were analyzed by doing psychological autopsies—bringing all the disciplines together to talk about what events and situations took place weeks before that may have led to the inmate suicide in question. The only single behavior that surfaced consistently as a strong predictor of suicidal behavior—and one cannot always determine this because so much depends upon the cooperation and openness of the inmate-patient—was that the inmate-patient had a real or perceived loss, total loss, of a folk-support system. The perception was that nobody in their lives cared about them, loved them, or would be there for them ever again. As an example of this, one inmate was a Russian who was deathly afraid of being deported to Russia after completing his sentence in the United States. He knew that once his sentence was over, deportation was going to happen to him. And apparently, going back to the Russkies for something criminal he had done there, he knew he would not be met with a prison sentence as soft and easy as he found in America. He finally succeeded in killing himself.

"Back in the late 1800s, sociologist Emile Durkheim wrote a seminal work concerning suicide in which he spoke about one of the main causes of such action, being the fact that people feel like they're literally alone, and there is no one there for them, a concept he called "anomie." That helps us understand how important the folk-support system is, even for people with Axis I and Axis II disorders. This reality was repeatedly borne out by numerous psychological autopsies following inmate suicides in prison."

Doc B. took the baton from Sam and continued the training: "In Centerville State Prison, there once was a female psychologist, Dr. Betty Grissom, who also would have scored high on the 'misguided benevolence scale.' She was a very pleasant person and quite bright but really did not get the picture about sociopathy and some of the dangers involved with it and the true character of some of these incarcerated individuals. After some time, consulting in the mental-health unit, she announced to her inmate-patients that she was leaving prison work and going on to a different position. One of her inmate-patients, who had been a drug addict and a real predatory and assaultive individual out in the free community, Damien Stabler, took offense to her announcing her leaving. He came up to the mental-health unit for an outpatient session and was, as per regulation, patted down.

"When inmate-patients come into the mental-health unit for outpatient counseling, they get what is called a pat frisk for weapons or any other contraband. They are patted under their arms, around their legs, and around their body. When a patient is admitted to the psych unit to stay there on an inpatient basis, the staff does what is called a strip frisk. That means all of an inmate's clothes are removed and a careful and complete examination is done of their body, their hair, their mouth, their anus, everywhere conceivable, even between their toes, to see what they might be carrying or hiding in the way of contraband. But outpatient counseling only required a pat frisk. Therefore the COs pat frisked inmate-patient Stabler but missed the fact that he had a razor blade taped to his chest, between his breasts, and he had another razor blade taped under one of his arms. Somehow the pat frisk missed the presence of these razor blades. Stabler got into his session, and asked Dr. Grissom if she ever thought about dying. He then leaped over the desk and starting cutting her face, her ear, her breasts, and started banging her head against the wall. Fortunately a correction officer, Andrew Shaw, was nearby and saved her. He pulled the sociopathic inmate-patient off her, subdued him, and locked him in a cell. The female psychologist had to be treated in a hospital and had a serious concussion, including serious swelling of her brain. Mental-health staff recalled talking to Dr. Grissom on the phone about a week later, and she was still talking very tentatively, sounding almost like a child. Dr. Grissom did not exhibit sound cognitive functioning at that time, but eventually, she got it back.

"Then, Dr. Grissom approached the district attorney in the county where the prison was, and she wanted to have an attempted murder charge placed against her attacker. One must remember that this was a woman who previously had some idea that these poor inmate-patients became the way they were through unfortunate circumstances in their lives, perhaps because of the influence of the neighborhoods, and they did not have much control over making positive changes in their lives. She foolishly underestimated the majority of convicted felons' penchant for vicious, predatory behavior. But now, faced with reality, she was looking for an attempted murder charge against her perpetrator.

"How the tables turned when she became the victim. The D.A. told her that, under the circumstances, the most he could charge the perpetrator for was first-degree assault, which was a very serious charge. Unhappy and angry, Dr. Grissom screamed and hollered at the D.A.—a total about-face for someone with these misguided benevolence leanings. She proved to be a great example of that. It's too bad more people who think that the system is too tough on inmates cannot see the truth without having to go through some disastrous personal victimization in order to learn. Dr. Grissom ended up leaving the prison scene, because she really could not work in that environment. She returned to private practice. Thank God she recovered, seemingly completely, from her wounds and from her head injuries. Anyway, as one can see, inmates in a maximum-security prison are very resourceful when it comes to acquisition and use of weapons."

Doctor Barilla remembered out loud: "A few years previous to Dr. Grissom's traumatic victimization, a couple issues occurred that are related to her situation and also drove home the reality that the *preeminent business in correctional work is security*! It's not education or mental-health treatment or family visits or vocational training or spiritual enlightenment. Initially after becoming forensic unit chief, I requested and received modification of the solid metal doors at the entrance to all clinicians' offices. Maintenance personnel cut out two-foot by three-foot openings and installed transparent plexiglass windows in those openings so that COs could patrol and observe, from a quiet distance, clinicians' sessions with inmate-patients on the unit. Each office desk had a hidden red alert button to summon immediate CO assistance in the event of threat or danger.

"Psychologist Brian Wagner was another staff member possessed of a high level of misguided benevolence at times. He seemed to be fascinated, delighted, and even admired inmate-patients' stories of predatory, felonious behavior. I caught him standing over COs, with an arrogant, disapproving glare, as the COs pat-frisked his inmate-patients, who regularly complained about this procedure, coming into the psych unit for outpatient treatment. My response was one of the few times I lost my cool and loudly berated a colleague who I clearly told was behaving highly inappropriately and was on thin ice with me. In fact, I strongly encouraged him to seek a mental-health environment for which he would be better suited. I narrowed the scope of his duties and maintained vigilance of his professional behavior until he ultimately chose to seek employment elsewhere. There was some evidence that he used illegal drugs, at least recreationally, and he had mostly chaotic relationships in his personal life. In our psych services, he managed to alienate colleagues regularly, but short of justification for termination. The important point in all of this is that *security* is—my Latin is a little rusty—the *sine qua non* (can't do anything else without it), of correctional work among *all* disciplines, not just uniformed staff."

After a particularly difficult day in mental-health services, lead CO Sherbach and Doc B. looked at their very cooperative, elderly, Hispanic inmate janitor and said, "Good jail, huh, Ricardo?"

The porter smiled enthusiastically and emphatically responded, "Good jail! *Da best!*"

Chapter 6

Stories from the Front Lines: When People Think They've Heard It All, They've Only Just Scratched the Surface

At this point in time, Dr. Barilla really thought that he had seen it all. With all his years of experience at the hospitals and in private practice, and especially, in the state-prison system, every unusual experience that had taken place led him to believe that he had witnessed more anomalies in personality and behavior than those witnessed by most psychologists. But, in truth, he had only just scratched the surface. Every individual who enters the mental-health arena has quirks, kinks, and character flaws, sometimes beyond the imagination. It is not enough to say that there are variations of similar psychotic events in persons with mental illness. Rather every situation is unique in its own peculiar perspective. No two cases are ever exactly alike. Doc B. often recollected examples of what he had seen in order to enhance his understanding of the range and depth of the human experiences encountered in his work, like a mosaic or a gestalt.

One time, there was an inmate strike at Centerville State Prison. Reportedly, inmates did not like the food or medical services, and they refused to work or participate in programs. The administration told the civilian employees to go home because security was just keeping a watch on the prison during the period of the strike. On his way home, Doc B.

went to his mechanic to talk about his car. The mechanic happened to be a Cuban guy, Cesar Velez. He was very friendly, and he asked Doc B., "What're you doing home so early?" Dr. Barilla told him that the inmates were striking and Cesar responded, "Oh, my gosh!" And then Cesar began to tell Doc B. a little bit about his background and his life in Cuba.

Cesar said, "I first fought in Cuba with Castro against the existing government, and then, when Castro gained power, I fought against him when I realized what he was really about. I was captured and put in a prison in Cuba where the prisons in some cases were like old Spanish forts."

Cesar continued, "During my imprisonment, the conditions were horrible: many men in a cell, no bathrooms, and only bread and water for nourishment. One of the inmates decided to get up a petition. As a result, the warden of the prison invited that inmate up to the top floor of the prison and the security staff took all of the other inmates and placed them outside the confines of the prison to observe. The prison officials took the petition from the inmate who had circulated it and shot the petition full of holes, then threw it over the side of the prison for the inmates to see. Then security forces shot the inmate petitioner full of holes, and threw him off the roof of this Spanish fort and into the moat which surrounded the prison, for all the other inmates to see. No one ever did a petition again."

Doc B. reflected to himself, "This is what is called one-trial learning and is another example of vicarious learning. As bad as the conditions were in the Cuban prison, when those inmates saw what the consequences were, they did not dare write another petition."

The Cuban mechanic just could not believe that inmates in a maximum-security prison in America would have a right to strike.

The prison system had a climactic event when Dr. Barilla was relatively new in his career in a penitentiary setting. This was the corrections officers' strike in 1979, which lasted for sixteen days and created a lot of problems for inmates, civilians, and some corrections officers. Specifically, there was a small percentage of COs who volunteered to stay on and work—and were later ridiculed by their peers and called scabs—to manage the penitentiary. All of the prisons in the state were forced to operate on a minimally-staffed basis. Programs were limited, opportunities for doing a lot of things were limited; it was a big job just to get inmates, who needed it, to sick call to make sure that all inmates were fed and housed, and to make sure that the staff was able to keep a lid on the behavior of inmates. There was frustration and concern of all involved to avoid a riot while the corrections officers, at least a great majority of them, marched outside the prisons around the state with picket signs emblazoned with the word, "Striking."

Civilians and, specifically, mental health civilians, had to go to other places; for example, Dr. Barilla was transferred to a facility that dealt with mental-health treatment for suspects facing felony charges but who were incompetent to stand trial. Detainees had to go back and forth to court once they were believed to be competent to stand trial, or they were held in this particular security-treatment hospital and treated for mental and emotional problems until they were competent to go back to court and actually stand trial.

In a private conversation in the mental-health unit, Doc B. recounted to Captain Rauch:

"A lot of us mental-health staff were in positions that were awkward doing things which we never did before. We civilians actually had to act like corrections officers in some situations and give orders and tell inmate-patients to line up, and keep the noise down, and things that were very uncommon or not traditional for civilians to do with convicted felons, or suspected felons, facing criminal charges. It turned out that the civilian employees who were minding the store in prisons, were diverted to work in these security mental-health hospitals. This involved working sixteen to twenty hours per day, getting very little sleep, and getting very little opportunity to do proper hygiene. There were periods during the sixteen days when personnel became so fatigued that they had to be relieved.

"The personnel were brought in and out of the prisons, or in and out of certain of these institutions housing suspected felons or convicted felons, by helicopter. That was challenging because many employees feared crossing the picket line either entering the facility or leaving the facility as that could actually start a serious riot. Those were some of the conditions surrounding the sixteen-day period as well as the fact that there were a lot of hard feelings from the corrections officers' union point of view."

Captain Rauch acknowledged that the COs felt that they weren't getting the proper benefits and the proper pay and the proper raises. These are common themes that have occurred in public service over the years whether one worked in government agencies, VA hospitals, or any kind of government-run facility. When the budget got tough or tight, government employees weren't getting very good raises or no raises at all.

Doc B. continued, "One of the measures of security for the security-treatment hospital for suspected felons facing charges was when the state brought up big-city detectives to guard the perimeter of one of the major buildings housing employees on the hospital grounds. Some corrections officers who were striking were threatening those who stayed behind to work and threatening the wardens of the prisons, none of whom were out on strike. As you know, Captain Rauch, most of the high-ranking officials at the rank of lieutenant and above stayed in the prison and did not support the corrections officers' union to strike."

There was actually a law which forbade any government employee from striking, and the corrections officers were threatened that they would lose two days' pay for every day that they were out and refused to work. They could be fired, and if they did anything crazy or violent, they could be prosecuted.

At the next think-tank meeting, Melissa Cochran, a visiting doctoral student, was curious about various stressors and leaders during the strike. Doc B. was happy to satisfy her interests.

"In one case, there was a Lieutenant Adams who was admired by all peers and all people in corrections, civilian and uniformed personnel alike, as well as by inmates. He went down to the picket line because people were threatening to do something to his family, and he challenged some of the more outspoken people to come forward and try to do something to him or else just shut up and get back to the picket line and stop acting like cowards. Nobody would mess with this Lieutenant Adams, because they knew they would be in serious trouble if they tried something. These actions are also reminiscent of the phenomenon when some inmates are locked in their cells and they threaten other inmates or they threaten staff while the cell doors are all locked and everybody knows there's no movement that's going to be allowed. But when the cell doors open those people that yelled out threats, suddenly often become quiet and mild as a lamb. Such inmates are called 'cell gangsters'."

*****

During his career in the maximum-security prison system, Dr. Barilla also did some pro-bono work with corrections officers in crises, those who had marital problems, suffered from alcohol and drug addiction, and some cases even those who became suicidal. In every maximum-security prison, just beyond the state property, there always seems to be a popular bar that is very prosperous, where corrections officers would often go after leaving the job instead of going home. In these places, they would get drunk and complain about the warden, about the inmates, about the sergeants and lieutenants. They would just bitch and moan, instead of taking care of business and going home to the wife and kids and doing the normal things like shopping and going to Little League and other family activities. There were a lot of problems in those kinds of situations, some of which resulted in marital problems, financial problems, and high levels of work stress.

*****

New psychiatric nurses and psychiatrists were always fascinated about some of the unusual inmate-patient problems and appropriate mental-health interventions. Doc B. talked to them about seeming epidemics or copycat behaviors that would challenge the clinical and correctional colleagues in mental health care. At a briefing in the mental-health unit, Doc B. recounted many such events.

"And then, there were a number of swallowers among our patient case load—inmate-patients who would swallow things out of anger, from sickness, or to get attention, or to get out of general population. One inmate-patient swallowed eighty-plus sewing needles. Others swallowed spoons, razor blades, metal bars of various sizes, and what they almost always did was cover the objects they swallowed with masking tape so that there would not be any sharp edges to perforate their esophagus or intestines or stomach. In some cases, inmate-patients did have to have major surgery because big objects would stay lodged in their throat or in their stomach.

"One time, there were three of these swallowers who did this behavior around the same time. As mentioned before, most of these individuals just needed a lot of attention. It was frustrating for staff to have to deal with them. Out of a need for some comic relief, I wrote an essay, the basis for which were these three swallowers. The three of them just happened to be of various sizes, one being very small, one being very big, and the third inmate-patient being medium in size. I likened them to the three bears. So I wrote this essay in which the biggest inmate-patient swallowed the medium sized inmate-patient after the medium sized inmate-patient swallowed the little inmate-patient. It just got out of control, and now inmates were not just swallowing objects; they were swallowing each other and becoming cannibalistic. This was something, however, not too farfetched, having seen some examples of such acts over the years with some of the strange people who had been taken into custody and incarcerated. Sometimes the only way to cope with those types of situations is to utilize humor. And sometimes, looking at the actions of inmates in the course of their behavior can bring some comic relief from all this madness as well.

"Female CO Helen Williams has often told two humorous stories about her early corrections career. Once she was on duty to monitor inmates and families at a picnic in the main prison yard. Realizing that one inmate was not accounted for, she looked everywhere and finally found the inmate and his wife performing fellatio under a table. The CO impulsively yelled out, 'Get that thing out of your mouth!' On another occasion CO Williams drove through Concord, a city where many inmates chose to live on parole to avoid temptations to commit crimes in the bigger cities. She playfully yelled out, 'On the count!' to see how many parolees would act guilty, nervous and come to attention. A good number did respond in the expected manner on more than one occasion."

New psychiatric nurse, Anne ___'d, asked Doc B.: "Are all or most of our inmate-patients wild, out of control, and psychotic?"

Doc assured Anne that the majority of the case load, of 250 patients, was doing outpatient counseling, with some on psych meds, while the great majority were stable.

Doc continued, "I had an inmate-patient once who had never been hospitalized. He would just come to therapy and talk about some typical incarceration problems. He was a very laid-back type of individual with one exception; he had this bad habit of shoving a ballpoint pen up inside his penis, into his urinary track. This act somehow aroused him very much. He stated that he was not sure how it started, so I recommended that he see the medical staff to make sure there were no medical infections or concerns, and apparently there were none. I also suggested that this inmate-patient see the psychiatrist while the inmate-patient and I could work on extinguishing this odd behavior. I had no idea how long the pen-piercing behavior continued and there was no justification for forced treatment or forced medications with this inmate-patient. After a period of time, he chose to terminate outpatient counseling. It is not surprising that Vaseline was the best seller in the commissary in the prison because there are a lot of inmate uses for that product! It en led many inmates to pursue their sexual interests."

"What about the role of corrections officers in mental-health care?" asked Doctor Woo.

Doc B. replied, "Sometimes there is inconsistency on the part of the security staff working three different shifts, or even civilian personnel working different shifts in the medical and psychiatric departments. If they send different messages by letting inmates do certain things, or get away with certain things, when one shift is on duty and the other shift is not aware of these things, there can be some serious problems. Clear, collaborative communication is vital in every aspect of a maximum-security facility, especially for those in the medical/mental health arena. We have been blessed in mental health with excellent, usually long-tenured COs, who become our colleagues in inmate-patient care."

Another humorous issue was that a lot of staff in the prison, including Doc B. himself, would volunteer to be on the Media Review Committee to make sure that all that "short heist" material, the girly magazines that inmates would get, had some redeeming value and did not just appeal to the inmates' prurient interests.

In mock indignation, some staff would proclaim, "My God! How can they be allowed to be looking at those things!"

Of course, the staff just had to see them—just to make sure they were not too morally poisonous to the inmate population! It is amazing how many inmates received nude photographs from their girlfriends or spouses. A lot of times the staff in the mailroom, who were required to screen inmate mail, would find clumps of pubic hair in the envelopes that were sent to inmates, presumably for their own personal enjoyment.

Doctor Woo then asked Doc B. if he ever felt positive about an inmate's chances to succeed after release to the free community.

Doc B. said, "Yes, several times. Once I was in one of these subunits in one of the medium-security prisons nearby, where I was very touched by an inmate-patient leaving the prison and going out on parole. He had served a short sentence. He was kind of a doofus sort of fellow, almost likeable. His crime wasn't very serious, but he was very vulnerable and easily led. However, on the day he was released, I remembered looking out the window from my office and, outside the razor-fenced gate, was a whole gauntlet of about thirty people with noise-makers, yelling, crying, and hugging, as this inmate-patient walked out the front gate. As I looked out, I had tears in my eyes and I got choked up about this scene. All I could think about was, 'Wouldn't it be super if every one of these convicted perpetrators, when they got out, had that kind of support and love waiting for them?' They would have a hell of a lot better chance to stay on a straight path and avoid recidivating, in my opinion."

Nurse Boyd asked, "Are some prisoners afraid of others, like because of race, ethnicity, religion, or anything else?"

Doc B. said, "Yes, it might surprise you that another issue of concern in the prison on the part of the older cons is that they're shocked at how some of these youthful inmates coming in are so wild and unprincipled and undisciplined, impulsive, and have a hardcore sociopathic value system. What is meant by that is that some of the old-timers had honor among themselves and had to believe that when one gave one's word, he meant it. The old-timers would talk to staff and say, 'We don't know where these people come from, but man, they are dangerous,' and they did not like being around them. This kind of phenomenon actually caused more concern among the inmates, especially the older ones, than what they used to call the inmate-patients—bug outs—the people who would have psychiatric symptoms and would be somewhat chronic in their dysfunctional behavior in the prison. Inmate-patients used to scare other inmates at times until this new breed of young inmates arrived: now the old-timers were really concerned."

Another anecdote that Dr. Barilla's office manager, Noel Baratta, reminded him of, was about the Turkish psychiatrist, Dr. Hadjid, who has been spoken about in previous chapters. This doctor was really a good guy and everyone in the mental health and medical units loved him. He was excellent with the inmates, and he was really effective in providing mental-health services in the prison environment. However, he had a real problem with betting on horses. He liked the races, and he liked betting on them, and he would start his day by opening three horse-racing newspapers on his desk.

He would always kid Doc B. and say, "Hey, how would you like to double your money? Why don't you give me twenty bucks? I'm going to the track tonight and I'll bring you back forty."

And Dr. Barilla used to say to him, "Look, why don't you give me the forty now, and I'll give you a twenty and you can double it and put it in your pocket?"

Dr. Hadjid would get mad at his counterpart and say, "Ah, you're full of shit! Never mind!"

Dr. Hadjid would be talking to some Muslim inmates and, being Turkish, he would always tell them in his broken English, "I am Muslim, too!"

The staff often teased him mercilessly about that. When it was convenient, he would say, "I am Muslim, too!" to ingratiate himself to influential Muslim inmates.

Noel, the feisty office manager, offered another funny story about the lovable Dr. Hadjid, who was a bit absent-minded at times, and who one day he came to work with two different colored shoes.

"I told him about it. As he glanced at his feet, he took out his pipe, lit it, and, thinking that he had smoked all the tobacco, put the pipe back in his pants pocket. Suddenly his pants caught on fire. The staff quickly had to drag him into the bathroom and throw some water on him and get the fire in his pants put out. We never let him forget those odd behaviors! What do you expect from a shrink?"

*****

Captain Rauch popped into the Thursday morning think-tank meeting to instruct the mental-health team about the Adjustment Committee.

"The Adjustment Committee is like a mini-court within our penitentiary. When an inmate commits an infraction by breaking one of the rules, such as punching another inmate or throwing food in the mess hall, or being out of place, then he is locked up in his cell and is seen on the following weekday by the Adjustment Committee. The committee is usually comprised of one lieutenant, a uniformed corrections officer, and one civilian who, ostensibly, is the advocate for the inmate. For a minor infraction, the inmate might receive a couple of days locked up in a cell or he might receive a week locked up in a cell if the infraction is more serious. If the inmate assaulted someone or has contraband in his possession, such as drugs or a weapon, he would probably be sentenced to the Box in the Special Housing Unit, where he would be locked up for twenty-three hours a day, with one hour of recreation."

Nurse Adams of the medical department asked, "Has there ever been a correctional officer who was like a legend here at the Centerville State Prison?"

Dr. Barilla answered, "Maybe CO Sherbach, our lead officer, would have the best information about that?"

CO Sherbach gladly replied.

"There's one corrections officer many of us know who, during his career, went up the ranks from officer to sergeant, to lieutenant, to captain, to deputy superintendent, and ultimately became the warden of a prison. He then completed his professional journey as a consultant to the corrections department in the state capitol. That is how admired and respected this man was. He was a big ol' country boy, very laid back, but everyone just knew this fellow's strength, courage, and wisdom wasn't wasted. When it was needed, he was there. There was a humorous rumor that when inmates had to face him on the Adjustment Committee when he was a lieutenant he would arm wrestle them if they wanted to compete and show their stuff. And of course, if the inmate lost the wrestling match, then Lieutenant Pete

Sanders, might give him time in his cell or, being a pretty good-natured person, the good lieutenant might give the inmate a break and cut them some slack if the infraction wasn't very serious. Pete was just one of those rare people who was looked up to by virtually all the inmates and all the correctional personnel—just a very unusual guy with humility and modesty about his great ability, skill, and wisdom."

Doc B. thanked CO Sherbach and asked Melissa to offer some positive aspects of prison life.

She replied, "Contrary to what has been typically written about prison life, there are a lot of positive things that take place in a prison. When one has been working in a secure setting every day, it becomes evident how much activity there is that is not negative. It's like a bustling little community, like a village in and of itself. Inmates sometimes do not spend much time in their cells all day long because they are busy going to school, working toward getting their G.E.D. or working toward a college education, or working in the kitchen, or going to the auto shop, or knit shop, or furniture shop, or going to the law library to work on their case. They may have family visits, even being allowed private visits with their parents or their children, or conjugal visits with their wife in the trailer that's just outside the main building, but inside the overall compound, if they have kept their record clean.

"Most inmates are more physically fit and holistically well in prison than they were in the free community. Prison settings offer a wide variety of sports and exercise equipment to promote fitness and recreation. It's interesting to note that 'in the day,' when there was no sophisticated fitness equipment in prison, inmates had a common, single, effective exercise for building muscle and stamina. It was done with two empty number ten cans discarded from the mess hall, inverted on the cell floor, which the inmate used to do push-ups, hundreds in each day, with his legs extended and feet elevated on his bunk. Imagine the difficulty of this exercise, done hundreds of times each day. Just try it, and you'll see why we can appreciate its value at virtually no cost to inmate or prison authorities. It also illustrates the positive resourcefulness of inmates when they are so inclined. There's a lot of hustle and bustle in the corrections community. Many inmates take great pride in dressing neatly; they iron their green shirts and pants, and when they go out on visits they can wear dress shoes and dress shirts or casual shirts, and the only requirement is wearing their green pants."

Doctor Woo asked if there has ever been a successful escape from this maximum-security prison.

Doc B. enjoyed answering this one: "Although there have not been many escapes from the maximum-security prison, there was one time when a couple of inmates reportedly found a way to leave dressed in female clothing. Some visitors apparently brought these inmates extra clothes, which the visitors had hidden under their outfits, and the inmates changed into them and actually walked out the front gate. They were caught pretty quickly. The reason for the quick capture was because most of the inmates, especially from the inner city, were brought up by only their mother. Typically there was no father or other significant male figure present in their life during their developmental years. Therefore, the few who have escaped usually head directly toward their mother's house, often where police and corrections officials were waiting for them.

"I used to think to myself, 'Man, if I'm doing a life sentence for murder, and I have a chance to escape, I'm going to be sending my folks a postcard from Argentina or Austria or someplace like that. I would tell them, I love you folks, but I ain't goin' back to America because I don't want to do the rest of my life in that nine-by-eight crib!' But so many inmates do not have the wherewithal to be independent enough and resourceful enough in the free community when strictly on their own. They have been so dependent on their neighborhood and their caretakers and the people whom they prey upon and people they depend upon, that they just can't be autonomous.

"But the prison community, in some ways, is like any other busy community. When things are going okay and there's not any threat of a riot or escape or some other chicanery, one would think at times that it is just another community. Everything is right there: opportunities for work and education, and relating to families, and so on. Therefore, it is usually not the bedlam or crazy madness, terrible tyranny, and despicable conditions that many people think always exist in a maximum-security prison. And many inmates are allowed to have considerable personal property in their cells, and they make a concerted effort to keep their cells clean, for the most part. Of course, that is not true of every incarcerated felon. There are some who are very sloppy, and their negligence will result in bugs and roaches infiltrating their cells and the cellblock in general. But the majority of inmates have pride, protect their cribs, and will make sure that any food items are covered tightly so that no bugs can get in at their food, in their clothes, or in their cells."

CHAPTER 7

PUNISHMENT OR REHABILITATION: THE ROAD WELL-TRAVELED

Psychiatrist Dr. Thomas Szasz offered a provocative idea about punishment: "Punishment is now unfashionable because it creates moral distinctions among men, which to the democratic mind are odious. We seem to prefer a meaningless, collective guilt to a meaningful individual responsibility."

Dr. Szasz was a strong advocate of personal responsibility. An interesting person with exceptional intellect, his beliefs put him in a very controversial arena with many of his professional counterparts, as he took issue with the idea that mental illness was a disease in the traditional sense, wherein psychiatry and medicine tended in that direction.

As one who took the works of Dr. Szasz with an open mind, Dr. Barilla found that he, too, could not simply classify an offender as one who should remain in a state of punishment, in the traditional sense, versus one who might have the possibility of rehabilitation. Rather, he believed in punishment, defined as time-out procedures, and positive reinforcement, with both concepts adhering to their four basic principals—that would be the Behavior Therapy approach to rehabilitation. To Dr. Barilla, there was a dilemma between punishment and rehabilitation, which continues to this day in correctional settings, perhaps even more so. This is what Doc B. has called, "the road well-traveled," because it certainly appeared to be that way. To state the dilemma more clearly, traditional physical punishment was used for untold decades in prison and failed. In recent decades, ineffective attempts at rehabilitation, which emphasized inmate benefits and privileges while deemphasizing traditional physical punishment, had failed also to make a significant improvement in rehabilitation of inmates.

Although Dr. Barilla had a great passion about mental-health issues, he was cautious about listening to the opinions of others, especially opinions about the prison environment, because many of those who have expressed their professional opinions can only "talk the talk," as they never have "walked the walk," by actually working in a penitentiary. They never had a uniform on, never were on the front lines, or faced these kinds of wild and crazy crises that take place in a confined and controlled institution, which is different even from a civilian mental-health facility.

Doc B. loved to discuss and clarify issues of Cognitive Behavioral therapy with corrections staff and mental-health staff, including COs. On this day, at the think tank meeting, Doc B. got into Behavior Theory.

"Despite what critics might say, I think that prison, designed for punishment, can also be a place for rehabilitation. To me, this is a road well-traveled in any prison setting. Were it not so, I would not have chosen this venue in which to practice my profession. I have studied and learned that, beyond the realm of traditional physical punishment, there are two primary means of influence that can lead to rehabilitation: positive reinforcement in response to a situation or punishment according to behavioral psychology. Each of these is also connected to the tenets in Cognitive Theory—that how a person thinks influences his or her feelings and together the thinking and feelings influence one's behavior.

"Changing one's irrational thinking and changing one's negative feelings about a situation can ultimately influence how one reacts and behaves in that situation. The result is to change or modify negative human behavior toward more pro-social, positive, autonomous, effective, reciprocal human conduct. All of these improvements will allow perpetrators to get along better with others by falling into some reasonable compliance with societal expectations. Positive reinforcement is the reward system to advance appropriate behavior, and punishment is the negative deterrent system that is used when behaviors occur that need to be diminished or extinguished altogether."

"How do these concepts actually impact inmates' lives?" asked the watch commander, Lt. Dave Jeffries.

Doc B. continued his mini-lecture: "Defining this further, there are four principles of positive reinforcement and punishment that apply in both of these concepts. The first is *Immediacy*, which means that whatever will be the corrective response to a behavior, whether it's a reward or it's a punishment, it is important that the consequence takes place quickly, as close to the occurrence of the behavior in question, as possible. This is a learning-by-association process, which must be experienced by the inmate in order that that person recognizes the connection between the consequence and the behavior. If it is a positive consequence, there will be a tendency to want to repeat the behavior; if there's a negative consequence, there will be a tendency to not want to repeat the behavior. The impact would not be nearly as effective if the consequences, in response to inappropriate behavior, were not carried out immediately."

Nurse Mary Smith of the medical department asked, "Doc, can you give us an example?"

"Sure, Mary. For example, a youngster at home on a Monday afternoon breaks a window in the house when he was told not to play baseball in the yard. His Mom says, 'When dad comes home this weekend, you're going to get a spanking.' It does not work as well as making the disciplinary consequence occur immediately after the inappropriate behavior. Likewise, we try to get rule-breaking inmates in front of the Adjustment Committee as soon as possible. Likewise, rule-abiding inmates, are often eligible for various rewards, such as, increase in privileges."

Doc continued, "The second principal is *Contingency*. This means that the reward or the punishment occurs only in the wake of the target behavior in question. As an example, if an inmate is in the Box doing time in the Special Housing Unit and he calls one of the correction officers, 'motherfucker,' or says, 'you're an asshole,' or something like that, then staff might plan a corrective response only when that specific outburst occurs. Foul language is not as critical to correct as a barbaric behavior requiring the resources that would be necessary in response to an inmate throwing a cocktail made of feces, urine, and semen, where the actor might have AIDS and whose blood may have penetrated those bodily fluids."

Harry Jacobs, Corrections Counselor, spoke up, "Can you make that more clear for me, Doc B.?"

"Yes, sir. Contingency means that the corrective consequence is directed *only* at the target behaviors to be increased or decreased. In the event of serious, dramatic, barbaric, negative behavior, there must be an immediate and powerful intervention. When an inmate in general population, or in the Box, gets frustrated and is pissed off, he might have a real urge to put together this cocktail and throw it at somebody. However, if he is able to maintain his cool and is willing to deal with his frustrations by talking it out, by asking for help, that is when there is positive reinforcement, such as praise and encouragement, for appropriate behavior. The reward is contingent upon the inmate who, at one time, did this barbaric act but is now showing a very mature, controlled, effective and civil kind of behavior. This is what the administration wants to see in any inmate.

"It must be remembered that among all the other things that are trying to be accomplished in a penitentiary by those in charge is cultivating a sense of maturity, responsibility, and autonomy in these inmates, so that they can function in the outside world, not just in a prison setting. It can be very difficult because many of them have never experienced sound conscience development. Many inmates have a Darwinian approach to life—survival of the fittest. So there is a lot of hard work to do. Above all, it is imperative to impress upon the inmates that there are certain behaviors that will absolutely not be tolerated under any circumstances and that is why a powerful intervention is necessary at times."

Doc asked his audience, "Everybody okay so far?"

All nodded in the affirmative, and Doc B. continued.

"The third principal is *Effectiveness*, sometimes referred to as "size," which simply means that the punishment, in the case of very negative behavior, or reward, in the case of positive behavior, has to be something that has an impact on the recipient of the consequence. For an effective punishment procedure there has to be a consequence that the inmate does not want to happen to him. For example, let's say there is an inmate doing a life sentence for murder and, while in the Box, he assaults another inmate or a correctional officer. Let's say he's already doing a lot of time in the Box, and he is told, 'Okay, we're going to take you to the Adjustment Committee. We're going to give you three more years in the Box.' This hypothetical inmate might not care at all. But, if you take away privileges that are very important to him, such as having no coffee, no cigarettes, no books, no personal property, no visits, and just let him sit there in his cell for twenty-four to seventy-two hours, contemplating what he did, this consequence might deter the inmate to limit or prevent such future assaults.

"With these types of consequences, called punishment by contingent withdrawal, most inmates typically feel disempowered. They feel emasculated. They feel humble. And they can't talk all that trash and do cell-gangster stuff like threatening, 'I'm goin' kill some motherfucker.' They are sitting in that cell, totally without any power, and very few resources, just sitting there thinking about what they did, twenty-four hours a day, for whatever period of time designated as the punishment.

"Most of the inmates in that situation improve their behavior significantly. It is very effective. In that period of time, they seem to have gotten themselves together and often promise they will go back to general population, or even remain in the Box, and they will desist and refrain from these kind of barbaric behaviors.

"They are told, 'If you repeat the behavior, you will be back in this situation in a minute and we might lengthen the conditions next time. We might send you to the mental hospital next time because we suspect you might be losing your mind to keep doing this barbaric, crazy stuff.'

"Now, when they go back to their regular housing or remain in the Box, they are followed up by the officers and the mental-health staff doing routine rounds. If they are maintaining their cool and refraining from barbaric behavior, they are praised for their positive change.

They are told, 'You're really getting it together. We're proud of you. Keep up the good work. We'll help you as much as you can when you're frustrated, when you're depressed, when you're upset. But the strategy you used before is out of the question. And you need to remove that strategy from your repertoire of dealing with frustration, because it's going to be more trouble for you.'

"The important thing is that when the administrative staff and health staff say those things, they really mean it. The praise should be sincere. Likewise, staff should not make idle threats in the penitentiary with these kinds of interventions. That's also part of the effectiveness. Taking something away from an inmate temporarily, is typical punishment by contingent withdrawal—it's like a time-out procedure. Applying the positive reinforcement, in the event that pro-social, civilized behavior has resulted from the inmate, has to be something that the inmate really appreciates and sees as rewarding, because this type of positive consequence builds up their confidence and helps restore their pride and can possibly make the real, lasting changes in their behavior."

Dr. Barilla suggested, "Let's take a moment to clarify the concept of punishment from the perspective of behavioral psychology. Please understand that there are two types of punishment. The first is Aversive Stimulation, which is physical punishment, like beating a person or hosing people down. The second is Contingent Withdrawal, which I've just explained. To bring the latter into a more recognizable forum, it is the kind of action used in the raising of children or by people in the work environment. For example, when an employee is perpetually late for work and the boss pulls the employee aside and says, 'Okay, one more time, and I'm going to send you home and dock you a day's pay. If you do it two more times, I'm going to send you home and dock you two-day's pay. The third time it happens, I'm going to fire you.' That's when it really hits home because it will affect the man's pocketbook—something they absolutely do not want to happen to them.

"That kind of contingent withdrawal works! When an employee starts coming to work on time and doing his job, he should get praised by being told, 'I knew you could do it. I knew you had it in you. Thank you for being a part of the team.' When that is done appropriately and sincerely, it can turn someone's behavior around."

CO Brinkley asked, "You staff people have to remember all this stuff when you do helping interventions? Wow!"

Doc responded, "Yah, if you want it to work, you do.

"Let's continue. The fourth principal is *Satiation/Deprivation*. Satiation just means that if someone really likes and appreciates a certain kind of reward, but they have been inundated with that reward, then they are less likely to perform the desired behavior. It's an unfortunate reality that often times an organism—human beings included—in a state of deprivation of something it wants very much, is more likely to perform the desired or mandated task than someone who is satiated. There is no reward in giving the latter more of the same, whether it's chocolate chip cookies or a pat on the back.

"Another way to describe the fourth principal, Satiation/ Deprivation, is that there is an excess of rewards in the case of satiation, or there is an absence of the rewards in the case of deprivation.

"At one time when I worked in a penitentiary with a Korean psychiatrist, he told me that he had been in the Korean army where high-ranking officers deliberately gave the troops less food, until they performed the mandated tasks. It was only then that they rewarded the troops with good meals. In America, that is something that could be considered unethical and all kinds of watchdog groups would be screaming unfair treatment or influence.

"The CO staff in the penitentiary were frustrated by the surveillance video cameras installed in the Special Housing Unit and in the elevators, and many COs claimed that, 'Some of these assholes could spit on, punch, do all kinds of things to the corrections officers, but there could be no retaliation or the correctional officer would lose his job!' So it was a real morale killer, until mental-health staff came up with some creative strategies to intervene, which were really humane and very effective as well."

Jim Barnett, deputy superintendent of programs, asked Doc B. a tough question: "How do you set up an approach or treatment plan to help an inmate improve mental, emotional, or behavior problems?"

Doc responded, "Great question; tough to give an easy answer. In the business of behavior management, behavioral change, and treatment planning, there is another approach that is very, very effective, but difficult to do because it requires a lot of hard work. Most people do kind of a watered-down version. The experts call it SMART. It's an acronym that stands for Specific, Measurable, Attainable, Reinforced, and Time.

"Mental-health practitioners should try to target a specific behavior they want to increase, change, or decrease. Examples might include positive pro-social behavior, such as somebody controlling their temper, somebody coming to work on time, somebody being a better listener. The practitioner must define and focus on that specific behavior and not just general behavior, such as someone who wants to be a nicer guy or someone who wants to get along better with people. Those behaviors are just too general. As an example of someone trying to change a specific behavior, they might say, 'When someone talks to me, I will listen for three minutes without interrupting.' That's very specific. Now it becomes necessary to observe and measure that behavior, so it has to be measurable as well. For example, if I'm trying to be a better listener without interrupting, I (or someone else) can time my patience and my courtesy by letting someone talk and see if I can make it for three minutes.

"This is where the 'A'—Attainable—is also a factor. Whatever the goal behavior is, whatever the target behavior is, it has to be attainable for the individual working on that issue. For example, I can't say to somebody, who has a very limited science background, that in one week I want you to be able to test and get a high passing grade in molecular physics. That would be ridiculous. But to listen to someone for three minutes without interrupting? For most humans, that is attainable. Some people are very good at listening, far beyond three minutes, and some cannot listen for three seconds without interrupting.

"So a goal has to be set that is attainable. If a person cannot achieve the goal because it's too difficult, then, in that example on listening, we would say to that person, 'Well, look, let's drop back—let's see if you can listen for one minute without interrupting or thirty seconds without interrupting.' A goal has to be set that is attainable because the person needs to achieve success and have a taste and experience of success. It is important for them to be able to produce a behavior that can generate a reward. This will give that person positive reinforcement that will strengthen their behavior and, perhaps, get them to push the envelope from thirty seconds to one minute in the example that we're using. Then it might be possible to increase the time from one minute to three minutes, in the listening example.

"Then comes the 'R' in SMART, meaning the behavior has to be Reinforced. It is imperative to positively reinforce behaviors that are highly desirable in someone who is not experienced in producing such a desired behavior. The purpose in all this is to turn a corner with these individuals—inmates in prison—to get them to learn and habituate a new positive kind of behavior.

"Finally, 'T' in the SMART acronym means this has to be accomplished within a designated period of time. To further explore the above example, we would not say, 'Well, listen, Joe, we want you to be a better listener. We'd like you to be able to listen for three minutes over the course of the next year. Can you do that?' This would be ridiculous, so a reasonable time frame must be set in which this goal can be accomplished."

Someone yelled out, "What about negative reinforcement, Doc? Isn't that the same as punishment?"

Doc said, "Great question about a common misunderstanding. The answer is 'No!'

"This is a good time to take a look at the category of negative reinforcement, another alternative, which is not as effective as positive reinforcement, but it does work. Contrary to popular opinion, negative reinforcement is not punishment. Rather it is a form of reinforcement, which in a subtle way promotes positive behaviors. There are some people who would use those terms—punishment and negative reinforcement—interchangeably. However, negative reinforcement is a tricky and interesting notion.

"For example, let's say I'm a kid in school and I like to wander the hallways and skip class every so often, but I'm scared shitless of the principal. Let's say that one day I'm roaming the hallways and I see the principal coming in my direction, but he doesn't see me. Then I run like hell to my class, and I get in there, which means I have effectively escaped the wrath of the principal. The behavior of escaping the principal's wrath, is reinforcing the behavior of appropriately attending class. But behind it is the fear of what the principal will do to me if he catches my butt out in the hallway. Escape is one form of negative reinforcement. Avoidance is another form of negative reinforcement, and it is somewhat connected to the escape paradigm.

"To continue with the example, let's say I know when the principal is out in the hallway, walking around and patrolling the school, and I'm never going to go out there and try to cut class or fart around during those times. In essence, I would be avoiding any problem, because I know what's going to happen—I'll get suspended or I'll get sent home or my parents will be called. So knowledge of the negative consequence actually strengthens my attendance in class and avoids disciplinary problems.

"Negative reinforcement is not as powerful as positive reinforcement because positive reinforcement occurs with an individual deliberately tries to do something appropriate and is then rewarded for it, but they do not stop doing a *preferred* inappropriate behavior, just to avoid problems or punishment. A perfect example of negative reinforcement in correctional work is when a CO yells out the command, 'On the count,' and every inmate complies immediately because they know the dire consequences of noncompliance. In behavioral psychology terms, the threat connected to noncompliance serves to reinforce the appropriate inmate behavior, namely, returning to one's cell, which is not something an inmate wants to do."

Nurse Boyd called out, "Hey, Doc, couldn't positive reinforcement apply to this situation?"

"Yes, and here's how it works. Hypothetically, when the inmate returns to his cell, he immediately receives some form of reward or positive reinforcement, such as extra yard time, extra visitation time with loved ones, credits toward gaining access to the honor block, or credit toward reduction of time served, if this process works properly. With ongoing praise and encouragement to the inmate, external rewards are gradually diminished, and a form of intrinsic reinforcement can occur; that is, the inmate might acquire a strong sense of responsibility and pride in doing the expected proper behavior."

"That's crazy! How can that possibly work?" shouted out one of the CO staff. Already the looks on other peoples' faces showed total disbelief.

"Remember," replied Dr. Barilla, "two basic simple rules. The reward has to be meaningful and desirable to the recipient, and the punishment has to be something that the recipient does not want to happen to them. The rewards of increased yard time, increased eligibility for the honor block, increased visitation time with loved ones, and reduction of time served, are all, obviously, meaningful to inmates. What is subtle and powerful and the very essence of rehabilitation is the gradual transformation of the sociopath into an individual with conscience, honor, and responsibility. Is it possible? Yes. Is it likely to happen for most inmates? Not likely, even under ideal conditions. Would the Department of Corrections ever set up such a paradigm to consistently reward inmate compliance? Possible, but not likely. What then do we do? Let's use the resources we have and help the motivated inmates to the best of our ability."

Nurse Conway, of the psychiatric satellite unit, who was very skillful in managing manipulative inmates, asked an important question: "Is reinforcement the same for everybody? Does it always come from someone else?"

Doc B. asked a visiting doctoral candidate, Melissa Cochran, to handle this one. Melissa gladly spoke on this topic: "There are some principles that are important insofar as reinforcement is concerned; however, they are not always applied very well. When a person begins reinforcing somebody to achieve a change in their behavior, the effect is usually more powerful if the process starts off with some kind of extrinsic reinforcement. This means that it is coming from outside of one's self; that is, someone is praising the person for a job well done or is praising that person for making a good effort to get to class on time, and so on. This is an interesting and subtle notion in behavioral management and behavioral modification.

"Over time, with the continuation of this extrinsic reinforcement of praising somebody for a job well done, pride is instilled that comes from taking charge in one's life and in doing things one is supposed to do. The result is the hope that one day the person in question will start to feel rewards coming from within one's own self. Extrinsic reinforcement can then lead to intrinsic reinforcement, which is feeling proud, feeling sometimes kind of free and autonomous, and taking charge of one's life by doing the things that are supposed to be done.

"The individual who is changing tends to feel good about being a person who is becoming more mature, competent, and self-reliant. These two notions—extrinsic and intrinsic reinforcement—are powerful motivators. Unfortunately, there are people who do not even want to reward or praise others for doing something positive, because their comment might be, 'Well, they're supposed to do that—why in hell should I tell them they're doing a good job?' or, 'Why should I reward them?' "

Melissa continued, "Two other notions about reinforcement that are also important are, first, regularly or *continuously* reinforcing the progress being made when a person is turning the corner and producing an appropriate behavior. Secondly, as the person seems to be taking charge and is being habituated in that appropriate behavior, issuing a reward *intermittently*, only once in a while, for a period of time, actually is more effective in producing the desired result. Then, at some point, the reward system can be eliminated altogether when a person has really taken charge and experiences all kinds of intrinsic reinforcement."

"Well done, Melissa!" Doc joined in.

"Let's digress a bit to the related, important topic of confinement as a form of punishment. Some years ago, Dr. Phil Zimbardo, a star in the field of psychology and a member of the staff at Stanford University, as well as a former president of the American Psychological Association, undertook a prison experiment at the college. He took twenty-six well-adjusted students and randomly assigned half of them to be inmates. The other half would be guards in a prison-like setting in the basement of a university building. They even had the help of the Palo Alto, California, Police Department to try to make it look realistic—the 'prisoners' would be arrested and handcuffed and charged with some criminal act. They would then be fingerprinted, given green prison garb to wear, and put in prison-type rooms that were fashioned after prison cells.

"The idea was to find out how dehumanizing the whole prison experience can be for both the prisoner and the people who work in the prison system. What happened was that the people who were the prisoners began to decompensate pretty quickly, partly because the people who were the 'guards' began to be abusive and began to really get intoxicated with power and doing punitive kinds of things with their so-called prisoners."

CO Sherbach from the mental health unit asked, "Doc, how long did this crazy experiment last?"

Doc continued, "This experiment was supposed to go for two weeks but had to be stopped after six days! After four days, one person became so totally decompensated as to be nearly psychotic, frightened, weeping, and depressed. The experiment came to a screeching halt."

Doc felt it very important to issue a caveat about interpreting the results of this experiment.

"The problem with this type of experiment is that, to draw an analogy from the results, it gives an erroneous conclusion because the inmates in a real prison—the sociopaths, the character-disordered people, the predatory people that come to prison—have had all kinds of experience through their lives in dealing with and preying upon people, committing crimes, doing time in juvenile lockup or adult prisons, and facing the courts. There really is not a legitimate comparison to be made here. The fact of the matter is that the prison experiment did have a dehumanizing effect on the well-adjusted students who were involved in the experiment. By contrast, the makeup of most incarcerated felons represents a lengthy, insidious desensitization process with regard to fear of police, jail, negative consequences, and gradual diminishment of conscience and empathy for others."

Melissa mentioned another possible analogy to incarceration: "There are times when one's home could be compared to that of living in a prison even though there are no physical walls or bars to separate one from the outside. The treatment that a family member receives can adversely affect the outcome of that person's life."

As Dr. Barilla gave thought to the number of influences that formed his life and work as a clinical psychologist, his mind continued to come back to the court case of sixteen-year-old Edward Hermann and the doctor's counseling sessions with Edward at the Monroe County Jail where Dr. Barilla worked as a consultant one evening per week.. Dr. Barilla, at this point, took some time to relate the Edward Hermann experience to the group. He described the gory details of Eddie's sinister plan, disturbing rationale, and execution-style shooting of his parents, older sister, and younger brother. Eddie's sister survived despite serious gunshot wounds, and she recovered enough to testify against Eddie at his murder trial. To outsiders, the Hermann family appeared to be an intact, normally functioning, middle-class family with two working parents and three kids in school.

It became quite obvious to Dr. B. that among the many factors contributing to Eddie's sociopathy were a cold punitive, tyrannical father, and Eddie's perception that he was a shunned middle child while his older sister was a spoiled princess and his little brother was the spoiled baby of the family. Eddie became a loner who worshiped the violent Rambo character from war movies and Eddie constantly wore battle fatigues. He regularly killed domestic and wild animals for practice and pleasure. Eddie was filled with rage and a perception of abandonment by his own family and most others.

Doc added, "To piggyback on Melissa's excellent point about family environments, it is our experience that strong, folk-support systems can positively impact the coping in prison and optimism for life after release of even the most hardened criminals. In our psychological autopsies of inmate suicidal deaths, we found that every inmate who took his own life had a real or perceived total loss of a folk-support system in which nobody involved in the deceased's life cared about them, loved them, or would be there for them."

As Eddie had said during his talks with Dr. B., it was not as if Eddie's father showed any love toward his family—he had no time for them, unless it was for something that he, himself, wanted to do. This characteristic, coupled with his lust for killing animals, whether for food or just for target practice, meant that Eddie's father provided no positive meaning in his family life, neither for himself nor for Eddie. They were, after all, just animals. Add to that the lack of his father's gratitude or compassion for Eddie's struggles in trying to please his father, and bond that should have existed between the two of them disappeared.

Doc B. continued to discuss some important lessons from the Eddie Hermann experience.

"When I continued in my interviews with Eddie, he often behaved normally, but with a cold, dispassionate air about him, like everything that had taken place was no big deal. I could understand, to a degree, his dislike of this father. However, it was when I questioned him about the rest of the family, I was shocked at what I heard.

"I asked Eddie, 'Why did you shoot your family? Why did you shoot your parents and your siblings?'

"He answered, seemingly without remorse or regret, 'They were on my back about my girlfriend, and my mother was always angry with me for not doing my homework. I hated them, and I hated my life at home!'

"That was a real eye-opener for me. I thought to myself, '*Good heavens! I've scolded my kids, and I've gotten on their case about not doing homework. Can this thing really happen in a normal family?'*

"It was after that, when I found out the history of this young man and his violent fantasies and his extreme antisocial behavior, that I discovered Eddie mimicked his father in so many ways. This horrific action by Eddie was not something that would be totally unpredictable—this kind of final, violent eruption that he planned and perpetrated. Eddie knew exactly what he was doing; he planned it; he did it with skill; and he was highly motivated to eliminate his entire family."

*****

Further regarding the subject of suicide, Dr. Barilla stressed the importance of doing a good screening of those who are being admitted to a penal institution. Doc instructed with emphasis about inmate-patients in this possible life-or-death dilemma.

"This is a time for establishing rapport with inmate-patients while getting to know about them and what is going on in their lives, both inside and outside the prison. Then, should an inmate have to be put on a close supervision suicide watch, which is usually constant for twenty-four hours, different shifts of corrections officers and civilians will literally watch the inmate-patient in that situation and take notes every fifteen minutes. The observing correctional staff will also restrict the inmate from any troublesome environmental situation, such as making a noose or banging their head against the wall, based upon the knowledge they now have about the inmate-patient. Those who are on watch duty really need to know how to talk to such inmates before, during, and after a suicide watch, because the suicidal inmate-patients, upon stabilization, are released and sent back to the general population. There may still be an immediate risk for a while and possibly a lengthier time down the road, depending upon how the inmate-patient's environment changes or how their thinking potentially worsens."

At the next think-tank meeting, Doc B. again called upon doctoral candidate, Melissa, to address the importance of good training for civilians working in the tough setting of the maximum-security prison. Melissa had actually worked for years in the past in prison as a master's-level psychologist.

"Where civilians take an active part in some of the prison work, it is important for them to understand a bit about the acculturation needed if they, as employees, are to interact with the inmate population. A lot of it is really common sense, but so many people come into the institutional environment kind of naively and have the attitude of the type of person who means well but who often has some level of misguided benevolence, to use Doc B.'s term. What they do not realize is that convicted felons, a great majority of them, can make people like them. They can go so far as to make somebody almost feel guilty as they prey on the uninitiated, so that these civilians might think, 'Oh my God, these poor fellows are doing time, and they are such nice people.'

"Civilian employees have not had the same benefit as the corrections officers, who typically have spent as many as sixteen weeks at a training academy where they have received extensive, specialized instruction on acculturation to prison life and getting to know the mindset of prison inmates. Following their academy courses, the correctional officers are then given on-the-job training in a maximum-security prison, so that they can really see the way life is in its most challenging surroundings. Then, when they get enough seniority, COs can make a bid to go to a medium-security prison or a minimum-security prison. However, a lot of the COs find that they enjoy the challenge of working in a maximum-security prison and actually remain there."

Melissa continued to address the issues in proper civilian training.

"Now, as far as civilians are concerned, they need a strong orientation to the prison community, including the problems, the services, the mission, and the rights and legal issues of inmates. They need to understand the traits of sociopathy with emphasis upon the inmates' tremendous skills and how they will work the system to their own advantage. They need to understand that the inmates' rap sheets—their records—really are only the tip of the informational iceberg for a lot of these convicted felons doing time. Members of the correctional staff need to remain firm, fair, confident, and assertive and always be team players when dealing with inmates. If there's ever any doubt about anything, then the inmate needs to be put on hold while the civilian checks with experienced colleagues as to how to proceed. Staff in these positions need to believe the basic worth and value of the inmates, while still holding them accountable and asking them to take full responsibility for their crimes and their antisocial behaviors. Above all, the inmates need to learn to feel and express remorse for their crimes.

"In addition to this, the inmates need to develop lasting conscience-driven, pro-social, law-abiding kinds of behaviors, without any excuses, because they will find excuses anywhere and everywhere (such as, 'it's the man'; 'it's society'; 'I was in the wrong place at the wrong time').

"Here's a typical scenario: 'Yeah, but Mr. Smith, it says here you were found surrounded by three dead bodies. You killed three people.' Mr. Smith's typical response, 'Yeah, that was just a misunderstanding, Melissa!'

"Finally, staff needs to see evidence of some kind that inmates are forming positive, supportive relationships and connecting with family and others in the prison, whether volunteers, religious people, or educators who really seem to be helping the inmates turn their lives around.

"Of course, the acid test is always when inmates and inmate-patients get out into the free community, and they are then left to make their own choices. And that is when people really find out what released inmates are all about, or if they can follow through on good intentions. Family ties are extremely important. Some of these inmates and inmate-patients just do not have these. They may have a single mother out there with whom they have a mediocre relationship. The sad thing is that, in life, everyone needs a folk-support system. So many young kids in minority neighborhoods join gangs because they have little or no family ties. The father may have left the home, and the mother may be on welfare or trying to work a job or has just given up and has turned to drugs and, perhaps, prostitution. The kids are left to fend for themselves, and they might befriend the local gang who tends to take them in as family. And that is where the crime problem accelerates."

"Terrific points, Melissa!"

Doc B. jumped in with other important information.

"Prison employees need the basic knowledge to utilize behavioral strategies; for example, how to use time-out procedures, when to give praise, and how to do both effectively. They also need to have a disciplined approach to the job while expecting the unexpected at any time. No one ever really knows with certainty what might suddenly happen in a penitentiary, especially in maximum-security. A normal day's activities for staff in a prison might include anywhere from five to ten crisis episodes during the day, probably three to four during the afternoon shift, and every once in a while, even one during the midnight shift with inmate-patients or somebody in the prison doing something that is construed as mentally or emotionally unstable.

"One has to learn to be cool under fire while dealing with a crisis. This is why good orientation is necessary for civilians; it should be under the guidance of an experienced corrections officer or staff member over a period from one to three years. It is highly risky when a new employee is thrown into work in a prison setting, especially maximum-security, without those basic requirements."

CO Sherbach suddenly spoke up and asked with a tone of skepticism, "Doc B. and Melissa, can we really do serious rehabilitation here in a max joint? Aren't there lots of roadblocks in our work here?"

Doc responded, "Absolutely! Let's talk about how our understanding the roadblocks can boost our limited success in the tough business of rehabilitating inmates. Some of the impediments to rehabilitation or effective punishment in the joint are that many inmates have never been 'habilitated' all through their developmental years, so the challenge of 'rehabilitation' with them is formidable, especially given the ineptitude, poor conscience development, minimal skill set, and lack of motivation to live within the mainstream of societal expectations.

"Liberal, influential forces in the penal system have seen fit to provide inmates with numerous services, benefits, and privileges without *earning* them! Meanwhile, inmates can refuse nearly any program, rehabilitative in design, while not incurring any penalty for their refusal, and they are still enjoying most of the same benefits as inmates who are striving to better themselves in the prison setting. Too many inmates abuse and manipulate the penal system to satisfy their own devious motives (they might rationalize it as survival) while those motivated toward positive change actively seek out programs, resources, and personnel which enable the rehabilitation process. With regard to 'punishment' procedures, nearly all of which involve time-out strategies as opposed to aversive-stimulation strategies, the major failings of these interventions can be traced back to insufficient understanding of and inappropriate application of behavioral-psychology principles as mentioned previously.

"One powerful and plainly stated principle is that prison authorities, especially treatment professionals, in order to correct inmate misconduct, need to know in each individual intervention what the inmate does *not* want to happen to him and *make it* happen, without shivering with uncertainty that the intervention could be misconstrued by certain critics as 'cruel and unusual punishment.' Equally as important, it is absolutely necessary to know what the inmate would find rewarding (that is legal, moral, and ethical), when that inmate corrects negative behavior and exhibits clear examples of appropriate behaviors. Inmates are people serving deserved prison time for their choices of criminal and maladaptive behaviors. It is also true that inmates are people with basic worth and value who, if motivated, can learn, change, feel pride and accomplishment, and embrace the often lengthy challenge of incremental growth in the law-abiding direction."

CO Sherbach yelled out respectfully and affectionately, "Wow, Doc! It's you and Mother Teresa, man! She ain't got nothin' over you!"

Doc smilingly retorted: "Thanks for the glowing compliment from my weird lead officer in mental health. Meanwhile, here's another important point to consider: The behavioral research is clear: punishment alone does not produce sustained positive changes in people, either in prison or in the free community. However, the effective use of punishment/positive reinforcement strategies requires knowledge of behavioral principles and knowledge of the person whose behaviors you wish to change. It also requires creative strategies with potential for success and a willingness on the part of all concerned to take some calculated risks to achieve the desired goals in the elusive business of rehabilitation. The road to prevention for adult, convicted, imprisoned felons is actually a road to *change*, since true *primary prevention* needs to begin and be sustained from the earliest developmental years under the benevolent guidance of all concerned. Not surprisingly, healthy growth and development, even at the earliest stages, also requires knowledge of, and appropriate application of, behavior-psychology principles."

CHAPTER 8

IN SEARCH OF PREVENTION:
THE ROAD LESS TRAVELED

At the next think-tank meeting, the warden opened with: "Doc B., the history of the dilemma—in what you referred to as the 'road well-traveled'—sure sounds frustrating! Can we discuss some ideas about prevention and effective correction in our treatment approaches, since traditional punishment and rehabilitation—as we know it—have not fared well?"

Doc B. happily responded, "Absolutely! The concept of a road well-traveled is not intended to signal hopelessness for making effective corrections to criminal behavior, when citing the historical dilemma, 'punishment or rehabilitation.' A number of experiments have been undertaken in an effort to find the right formula to correct and, where possible, to prevent such offensive and criminal behavior. The efforts of rehabilitation have often been impeded by the inmates' own makeup. Here are subjects who have been incarcerated because of their felonious actions. But how often have people heard the old adage 'An ounce of prevention is worth a pound of cure'? It seems that people have, almost always, taken the easy path of ignoring troublesome issues until, later on, such issues become serious problems demanding attention. When the concern is with civilized human beings, individually as well as collectively, needing to embrace societal mores, it is not wise to minimize the lasting potential effectiveness of sound preventive and corrective measures. In plain language, it is imperative that we address and correct the problems of antisocial behavior. Before I examine the reasons why this is so, consideration might be given to the wise words of the Joseph Malins poem, 'A Fence or An Ambulance' written in 1895, reportedly in support of the Prohibition Movement at that time."

Doc B. asked permission, and was granted, to read the poem:

Twas a dangerous cliff, as they freely confessed,
Though to walk near its crest was so pleasant;
But over its terrible edge there had slipped
A duke and full many a peasant.
So the people said something would have to be done.
But their projects did not at all tally;
Some said, "Put a fence around the edge of the cliff,"
Some, "An Ambulance down in the valley."

But the cry for the ambulance carried the day.
For it spread through the neighboring city;
A fence may be useful or not, it is true,
But each heart became brim full of pity
For those who slipped over that dangerous cliff;
And the dwellers in highway and alley
Gave pounds or gave pence, not to put up a fence,
But an ambulance down in the valley.

"For the cliff is all right, if you are careful," they said.
"And if folks even slip or are dropping,
It isn't the slipping that hurts them so much,
As the shock down below when they're stopping."
So, day after day, as these mishaps occurred,
Quick forth would their rescuers sally
To pick up the victims who fell off the cliff,
With their ambulance down in the valley.

Then an old sage remarked: "It's a marvel to me
That people give far more attention
To repairing results than to stopping the cause,
When they'd much better aim at Prevention.
Let us stop at its source all this mischief," cried he.

"Come neighbors and friends, let us rally;
If the cliff we will fence we might almost dispense
With the ambulance down in the valley."

"Oh, he's a fanatic," the others rejoined.
"Dispense with the ambulance? Never!
He'd dispense with all charities, too, if he could;
No! No! We'll support them forever.
Aren't we picking up folks just as fast as they fall?
And shall this man dictate to us? Shall he?
Why should people of sense stop to put up a fence,
While the ambulance works in the valley?"

But a sensible few, who are practical, too,
Will not bear with such nonsense much longer;
They believe that prevention is better than cure
And their party will soon be the stronger.
Encourage them then, with your purse, voice and pen.
And while other philanthropists dally,
They will scorn all pretense and put up a stout fence
On the cliff that hangs over the valley.

Better guide well the young than reclaim them when old.
For the voice of true wisdom is calling,
"To rescue the fallen is good, but 'tis best
To prevent other people from falling."
Better close up the source of temptation and crime
Than deliver from dungeon or galley;
Better put a strong fence round the top of the cliff,
Than an ambulance down in the valley.

The listeners remained quiet for a moment, and then suddenly, "Good analogy, Doc!" said a voice from the group.

"Yeah, what a great metaphor!" said another as most of the staff nodded in approval.

Doc B. smiled in acknowledgement and again called upon Melissa to speak, this time to address different notions of prevention. She happily obliged.

"Adult criminals seldom experience effective punishment or meaningful rehabilitation in modern correctional facilities. The best alternative is, again, finding the means for effective prevention. As mentioned before, the road to prevention for adult, convicted, imprisoned felons is actually a road to change since true, *Primary Prevention* needs to begin and sustain from the earliest developmental years. The 'Ambulance in the Valley' *is* a metaphor for *Tertiary Prevention*! What is meant by Primary Prevention is the use of proactive strategies, which effectively prevent undesirable problems from happening. *Secondary Prevention* indicates interventions, thought to be helpful in limiting the damage from problems that have already begun. Tertiary Prevention denotes more extreme and difficult strategies in an attempt to remedy significant problems, often described as crisis situations."

****

Many questions by staff bombarded Doc B. about the difficult transition for all concerned—all staff and inmate-patients—when the locations and delivery of mental healthcare changed in the mid to late-1970s. Dr. Barilla took a deep breath and began.

"Here's the story. In both the psychiatric hospitalization and treatment within the corrections setting and in the civilian psychiatric hospital setting the emphasis was on short-term patient treatment, with a lengthy, diverse, outpatient treatment program to follow, which allowed patients to assimilate into the general population or into a reasonably normal lifestyle. The belief began to emerge, through considerable experience and research, that patients suffering from various mental and emotional illnesses could actually enjoy a more normal, healthy, wholesome lifestyle, as long as those patients continued to receive outpatient mental health treatment.

"There was another lesser-known impediment to the smooth transition in the correctional system from lengthy inpatient treatment in a security hospital, to outpatient treatment in a correctional facility. Specifically, there were many psychiatrists and other mental-health professionals working in the pre-1970s correctional mental-health settings, who were not fully licensed or were only working under temporary licenses. For these individuals, the new system would require licensure in every discipline related to mental-health care in the new scheme of having a full-fledged community mental-health model, in maximum-security prisons. Also, there would be a reduction of the two hospitals for the criminally insane, now called security-treatment hospitals, to just one hospital for psychotic, convicted felons, receiving short-term mental-health care. Subsequently, the inmate-patients would then be returned to the community mental-health treatment models in a designated maximum-security prison."

The doctor continued, "When the delivery of ˇ ˛ental-health services changed in the mid-1970s, the task for mental-health care in corrections was given to the Office of Mental Health, Forensic Services Department. Many influential social activists and mental-health professionals had been concerned for years that mental-health services in the hospitals for the criminally insane were not adequate as provided by the temporarily licensed health professionals. Of equal concern were other conditions, such as corrections officers actually being responsible for the distribution of medications to the inmate-patients. Additionally, responsible mental-health professionals began to realize that many of the inmate-patients in the hospital for the criminally insane had strong Axis II disorders, especially antisocial personality disorders. Professionals also realized that many of these inmate-patients preferred to be in an environment where there was a greater degree of freedom and opportunity to engage in various kinds of antisocial behaviors. For example, there had been a high incidence of preying upon other inmate-patients, avoiding incarceration in a nine-foot by eight-foot cell, which is mandatory in correctional facilities, and finding ways to abuse the abundant availability of psychiatric medications.

"Among the numerous problems during the transition, many sociopathic inmate-patients began to act out when discovering, and when being told, that they were going to be transferred to a correctional facility to serve out their time. They were also told that they would continue to receive mental-health care in that correctional setting. Examples of acting out included inmate-patients threatening to commit suicide by actually cutting their arms and other parts of their body on the very day that they were scheduled to be transferred to correctional facilities. Among the more courageous and sensible psychiatrists, there were many cases of these acting-out inmate-patients being treated medically on the spot. These included administering sutures for various self-inflicted wounds and then placing the inmate-patients on the bus to deliver them to the designated correctional facility where they would continue to serve out their time."

"Doc B., did any person or group create serious opposition to all these difficult changes?" asked lead CO Sherbach.

Doc B. answered, "When the mandate for the transition of mental-health care in correctional settings was delivered to all concerned, there was some bitching and complaining by the rank and file, and people in authority. Most managerial and supervisory staff, including the wardens of all facilities, reluctantly had worked through the governor's office and through the legislature to accomplish this goal. The wardens, although skeptical, realized that they had to comply and had to adjust to the new system of delivering mental-health care in maximum-security prisons, and even in prisons of lesser disciplinary status.

"Everyone was concerned that the short-term treatment in the one centrally located security-treatment hospital would not be effective, and the general concern was that most emotionally and mentally disturbed patients, especially those with chronic problems, would create turmoil and havoc within the everyday operations in the maximum-security prisons. As the transition began to proceed, the leadership in correctional facilities, especially wardens, outwardly accepted the changes. But the scuttlebutt was that in private, among their peers, they had grave concerns about security and stability within the correctional facility. The memories of Attica riots in 1971 and other prison problems in the country were only six or seven years old, and nobody wanted to revisit those kinds of troublesome events. Overheard dialogue from some of the prominent wardens was that there was no way they were going to have 'fucking, bug out' inmates, chronically mentally ill 'space cadets,' wandering around their prison and creating more problems than they already had on a regular basis. The transition for mental-health care that was underway was especially difficult in the correctional settings, when one considers the long-established tradition that penitentiaries were designed only to punish convicted felons."

"Hey, Doc, how did all this change start? Did it just explode on the scene without much preparation?" asked CO Brinkley.

Dr. Barilla explained: "Some facilities, actually very few facilities, had somewhat of a forewarning of what mental-health care within the maximum-security prison would be like. For several years, before the actual mandated changes passed the legislature, in the Revere Correctional Facility, the emotionally and mentally troubled inmates were kept in A1 Company, on A Block. The mental-health department provided one mental-health professional a day, seven days a week, to come to the maximum-security prison, and to A1 Company specifically, to check on the forty-two inmate-patients living in that company, and to provide some sort of superficial counseling and support for them. This was done by professionals who had foreseen the likelihood that changes were coming and who believed that mental-health treatment on a larger scale could actually be provided in maximum-security prisons, despite the lack of history or experience in this regard.

"The quality of mental-health services, initially, was very superficial and very basic. However, those professionals involved were envisioning mental-health services beyond this infancy, to a much grander scale, in fact, very similar to established practices in civilian, community mental-health service. The corrections and mental-health leadership, with the advancement of these ideas and these practices, actually envisioned having a community mental-health model in every maximum-security prison in the state. That meant that they would have inpatient services, outpatient services, daycare services, and programming for chronically mentally ill inmate-patients. These ideas and these visions actually began to materialize and operate in 1977. The very superficial mental-health involvement in the early experimental days in the one maximum-security prison, mentioned previously, did not include all of the necessary aspects of professional mental-health care.

"The new system included secretaries, record systems, methods for providing scheduling on a regular basis, full professional coverage and services, and documentation of progress or lack thereof, with each of the inmate-patients. When the new system became operational in 1977, all of the staff and all program resources were in place and were functioning, so that mental-health care began to take shape fairly rapidly. The actual renaming of the small handful of mental-health professionals, probably about 150 in all, who managed and provided the mental-health treatment and care for convicted felons in maximum-security settings, adopted the title of 'Division of Forensic Services, Office of Mental Health.'"

Doc B. held everyone's attention and moved on.

"With the new 'forensic' system in place and with the knowledge that tertiary prevention was the most common type of mental-health/behavioral treatment, professionals needed to ponder possibilities. There was a need to examine what approaches were possible, effective, and rehabilitative in the correctional system, versus some of the approaches that had been proven historically to be ineffective, especially, in maximum-security prisons. It is perhaps interesting to note that research done from 1980 to 2002 in state prisons, indicated that the murder rate in prison dropped by 90 percent during that period, and suicide rates in prison dropped by 60 percent during that same time. That certainly promises the creation of a more emotionally stable situation within the correctional facility, but there is very little evidence to indicate that the recidivism rate, that is, the released inmates' behavior in the free community, has gotten any better. The recidivism rate continues to be reported as very high in most states."

Nurse Boyd interjected, "Do some program specialists claim credit for the reduced suicide and murder rates in prison? And do any of those specialists claim that their rehabilitation programs are superior?"

"Many so-called rehabilitation programs, when subjected to behavioral science scrutiny through appropriate methodology, have shown to be ineffective or not very durable in terms of changes in a criminal's life pattern. Among them is Scared Straight, a program that was devised in New Jersey's Rahway Correctional Facility. It proved to be effective for short periods of time with juveniles, but the interventions used in that program proved to be ineffective in terms of enduring positive changes over long periods of time, such as two years or five years from the termination of the program. Another such program has been called 'Criminon,' which purports to treat criminals' self-respect and claims that psychology and mental-health professionals in general, know nothing about what makes a criminal engage in sociopathic behaviors. There does not seem to be any known evidence that this program was subjected to scrutiny by the behavioral sciences to prove that it has indeed been effective and that the treatment has had a lasting positive effect on the criminals' lives. It is important that success occurs, not only within the correctional facility, but for many years beyond the criminals' release from prison.

"It is my opinion and experience that any rehabilitation programs, which can hope for reasonable success with imprisoned felons, would have a cognitive-behavioral orientation. A few such concepts and documented successes for positive change in people are found in Sharp's *Changing Criminal Thinking: A Treatment Program,*, Kohlberg's 'Stages of Moral Development' and Covey's *Seven Habits of Highly Effective People.*"

CO Brinkley yelled out, "What about the inmates' responsibility to make programs work?"

Dr. Barilla accepted the challenge, chuckled, and responded, "These and other potentially successful programs require the inmates' genuine motivation to persevere in treatment, and to expect only *incremental* progress in the beginning. It is also important for the inmates to embrace the practice of continuous, balanced renewal—mentally, physically, emotionally, and spiritually—throughout the remainder of their lives. Furthermore, potentially effective rehabilitation programs would benefit from studying former criminals who have become rehabilitated and are enjoying a lifetime of law-abiding success in the free community. Undoubtedly, some other important aspects of effective treatment include learning to strengthen family and church ties, improving educational and vocational opportunities, and strengthening conscience development. It's also important to note that such programs require the initial modification and elimination of irrational thinking and other cognitive changes that typically lead to successful management of one's emotional life and also lead to adaptive and pro-social behaviors. One must recall the important sequence of how our thinking influences our feelings and behavior."

*****

Dr. Barilla's ideas and suggestions, based on his and others' professional experiences, were reasonably well-accepted by the corrections and mental-health staffs.

Doc B. smiled, then frowned, when CO Sherbach and Captain Rauch met him privately and Sherbach challenged Doc B, "Jesus, Doc, how in the hell are we gonna do all that shit?"

Doc responded with a look of supreme optimism and said, *"Good jail! Good jail!"*

CHAPTER 9

QUO VADIS: WHERE DO WE GO NOW?

In his discussions with the students at Concord College and the correctional staff at the Centerville State Correctional Facility think-tank sessions, Dr. Barilla said, "References have been made throughout my narration of my journey through the 1970s about certain significant events, specifically, the Attica riot, change in the delivery of mental-health services, the AIDS epidemic among inmates, corrections-officers strike, and the murder of a female corrections officer. All of these events had a powerful impact on cultural changes in correctional facilities, especially in maximum-security, and the way life and business were transformed during the period from the early 1970s, through the early 1980s.

"Those significant events had the initial effect of creating turf wars, and many issues were divisive in terms of detracting from the unity or teamwork of the several different disciplines in corrections, such as parole, medical, corrections counselors, mental health, and uniformed personnel. However, it was also pointed out that correctional facilities began to experience healing and gradual resumption of unity among the corrections disciplines. Early on, some people from each of the disciplines gave their best effort to work as a team in the management and treatment of incarcerated felons. It took the passage of a period of time for others to follow and for correctional facilities to achieve effective unity in their mission of managing convicted felons."

*****

At a think-tank meeting at Centerville Correctional Facility, one of the new staff members called out, "Doc B, wait a minute! Tell us about the tragedy of the murdered female CO. Where did that come from? How did you and others handle it?"

Dr. Barilla felt obligated to tell the whole tragic story. Sadly, he proceeded.

"It is probable that the event that had the most dramatic and immediate impact on cohesion and cooperation of the many disciplines, was the alarming announcement on May 15, 1981, that Corrections Officer Denise Childs had missed roll call and soon was declared missing. The prison was locked down for ten days to search for the missing corrections officer and to investigate foul play. Ms. Childs' lifeless body was found in a dumpster on the prison site, and examination proved that, before and after death, she had been subjected to physical and sexual degradation."

The doctor continued to offer more sad details of the heinous crime.

"Criminal investigators who came to the Centerville State Prison to investigate the murder of CO Denise Childs, concluded that inmate Woodrow Lincoln had lured the female corrections officer into the Catholic Chaplain's office, after dayshift hours. Ostensibly he offered to show her some of his paintings in the hopes that she would buy one of them. It also appears, in retrospect, that this diabolical character, inmate Woodrow Lincoln, had worked his way into a position of trustee at the correctional facility. He was actually able to mingle with many civilians and correctional officers near the front part of the prison where security was not quite as thorough and intense as it was in the belly of the prison.

"It appeared that the sociopathic inmate had begun to befriend the targeted female corrections officer, and he picked a time and place that would be convenient for him to perpetrate the heinous crime. Not surprisingly, the facts and investigation indicated that inmate Lincoln had tortured and brutalized with biting, scratching, cutting, and beating the female corrections officer while she was dying and even after death! It appeared that inmate Lincoln then took the corrections officer's remains and stuck them in a plastic bag and placed her dead body in a large garbage dumpster, which was eventually, unknowingly, moved by other inmate workers to the waste dump on the prison property.

Searchers found the body of Corrections Officer Denise Childs in the prison dumpster after ten days of lockdown and investigation. When the mutilations on her body were discovered, a bite expert was brought into the investigation. Fairly quickly inmate Woodrow Lincoln became the prime suspect in the brutal murder. He was arrested and tried in the local county court, which subsequently found Lincoln guilty of first-degree murder. The jury sentenced him to die in the electric chair, despite inmate Lincoln having the benefit of a prominent lawyer.

As it turned out, the governor believed that executing Woodrow Lincoln was unconstitutional, and he vetoed the use of the death penalty for this hardened criminal."

It seemed that the entire prison, as well as the prison system, was greatly shaken by this one horrendous act, the first time in a northeastern state that a female CO on duty had been murdered. During the investigation and trial of inmate Lincoln, everyone had something to say, including Dr. Barilla, who was accosted and asked for explanations by numerous staff at the Centerville Correctional Facility. It was almost immediately after the discovery of CO Childs' body and the events leading to her murder that Dr. Barilla happened to run into Captain Rauch, whose first question was, "What do you think of all this, Doc?"

In their private conversation, Doc B. sadly responded: "The heinous murder of Corrections Officer Childs is a culmination of a correctional system gone awry, to the point that it is a system that is neither fish nor fowl—not punishment and not rehabilitation. Ten years after the Attica riot, there has been a continued diminishment of punitive strategies and an insidious increase of misguided benevolence toward incarcerated felons in the form of increased rights, increased benefits, increased and tolerated inmate opposition to beneficial programs, and inmates' increased sense of entitlement—all feeding nicely into the antisocial personality persona! It's the proverbial cart before the horse: the reward generously bestowed *before* the inmates' genuine efforts to produce pro-social, law-abiding, behaviors. Such achievements, by inmates, need to be witnessed and documented, by those who *should* know the real from the contrived! Remember behavioral principles, especially *contingency*! We don't give the reward until the desired behavior is produced and documented by an appropriate authority!"

"Geez, Doc! Let it all out. You're not holding anything back are you?" quipped Captain Rauch sarcastically.

Dr. Barilla responded quickly, as though he had to spit out his bottled-up frustration, and he thought: *Piss on tact and diplomacy.*

"It's the ultimate failure of the rehabilitation system. What's wrong with this picture? A diabolical, repeat murderer, serving several life sentences, is accommodated to commit heinous murder again, while confined in a maximum-security prison, in the Chaplain's office, in front of the prison, in front of God and everybody else!"

The discussion between the captain and Doc B. had elevated in decibels just enough to draw a few more people in to listen.

Captain Rauch, who had become a reluctant convert to rehab programs in corrections, including mental-health care, lapsed back into his hard-lined stance.

"I told you for years: they're all mutts, losers, and gamers that you can *never* trust. They're fuckin' hopeless—with all due to respect to you, Doc!"

The doctor didn't have to think before responding: "Captain, despite my frustration and outrage, I believe in every individual's basic worth and ability to change. If I ever abandon that belief, I'll change my career!"

Dr. Barilla paused at length, saddened and feeling at a loss for meaningful direction.

"What can we do that will work? Where do we go from here? I seriously fear the status quo will be extremely difficult to disrupt or change. There are too many powerful forces exerting their will to maintain the failing system, and we've heard some of those people say, 'Something is better than nothing.'"

Dr. Barilla continued, "Where do we even begin? Are we like characters in philosopher Sartre's *No Exit*, a living hell from which there is no escape; in which we project *our* failings onto others and blame *them* for our failings?"

Dr. Barilla paused and peered at all present, who were witnessing the discussion with a look of renewed determination.

"In one respect, the perpetrator in this tragic event was not an active mental-health patient on psychiatric medications, a condition that probably would have been interpreted as a grave failure of mental-health care in the correctional setting.

"Many would say, among some of the more uncharitable comments, 'It's fuckin' crazy; mentally ill inmate-patients don't belong here! Never did!'"

Shaking his head and, then, inhaling a deep breath, Dr. Barilla made one final comment: "Fuck that shit! Let's roll up our sleeves and get back to work!"

*****

As it turned out, the events surrounding the brutal murder of

Corrections Officer Childs, the first female corrections officer in the area to die in the line of duty, served to strengthen the collective commitment of all prison personnel to work in harmony and greater vigilance to effectively manage prisoners in this maximum-security prison. It seemed that, along with the influence of other factors, a major shift in the prison culture had occurred, and there seemed to be a renewed sense of collective responsibility and professionalism.

After CO Childs' murder, and two months following the trial's conclusion, the warden of Centerville State Prison called the first of many meetings with leaders in the prison system, as well as higher authorities from the state capitol, and members of the watchdog Commission on Corrections. The state government sent a task force to Centerville State Prison to brainstorm about more effective approaches to rehabilitation and punishment in maximum-security prisons.

At that first meeting, Dr. Barilla was asked by Warden Mulligan to speak to the assembled task force.

Doc B. took the lead: "Among the abundant evidence supporting the value of cognitive-behavioral strategies used in efforts at rehabilitation, as well as the disappointing data related to failed efforts at rehabilitation in many recent decades in prison settings, are the data offered by a prominent criminologist and his colleagues. They researched the problems that exist throughout the arrest, trial, conviction, and incarceration of convicted felons.

"One researcher states, 'While official statistics show clearly that virtually all prisoners are violent or repeat criminals, for at least two reasons the actual amount and severity of crimes committed by prisoners when they are free are still many times greater than these statistics reveal! The first reason is plea-bargaining. Numerous studies show that over 90 percent of all adjudicated felony defendants do not go to trial, because the offender pleads guilty to a lesser charge. Countless crimes are swept under the criminal records' rug by plea-bargaining. The second reason is that most prisoners commit many times more non-drug felony crimes than the ones for which they are arrested, convicted, and imprisoned'."

Doc B. continued, "In two studies conducted in the early 1990s and published in the *Brookings Review* and the *Harvard University Economist*, two prominent authors found that the average (median) number of crimes, excluding all drug crimes, committed by prisoners the year before they were imprisoned, was twelve! The criminologist goes on to say that the data for the nation show that within three years of sentencing, nearly half of all probationers and parolees are convicted of a new crime or abscond. The researcher continues to say that, the closer one looks, the clearer it becomes that a huge fraction of America's crime problem results from lax probation, parole, and pretrial release policies (Remember? Violations of the principles when using punishment: *immediacy, contingency,* and *effectiveness!*).

"The researcher also alludes to statistics from the State of Florida in which he states, 'A 1993 Florida Department of Corrections study reported that between January 1, 1987 and October 10, 1991, some 127,486 prisoners were released early from Florida prisons. Within a few years of their early release they committed over 15,000 violent and property crimes, including 346 murders and 185 sex offenses! Most of these crimes would have been averted had the convicted criminals spent even 85 percent of their sentenced time in prison but, as the data show nationally, about half of all parolees serve 14 months or less in prison before they are released and spend well under half of their sentence time in confinement.' The data cited here only begins to scratch the surface of the inappropriate use of, or lack of understanding, of effective cognitive-behavioral strategies that can be valuable in managing and treating convicted felons, in a maximum-security prison."

*****

Dr. Barilla focused on data even more relevant to mental illness in the context of crime and incarceration: "To turn to another considerable challenge within correctional settings, some authors allude to prisons becoming 'new asylums' because of the nearly 500,000 so-called mentally-ill men and women serving time in US jails and prisons. One author points out that, by contrast, fewer than 55,000 Americans currently receive treatment in civilian, inpatient psychiatric hospitals. The authors citing these data neglect to mention that it was through the questionable wisdom of influential leaders and mental-health treatment individuals (with misguided benevolence), who initiated the move to empty out the civil psychiatric centers, beginning in the late sixties and early seventies.

"It seems quite clear that many mentally ill patients were unprepared to deal with the various kinds of programs and halfway houses, once released from the major psychiatric centers. It seems unfair to blame the correctional system for housing inmate-patients who break the law and who probably are given many chances to correct their criminal behavior on probation. Naïve, influential groups with decision-making power in society, decided that chronically ill inpatients should be able to adjust and assimilate into life in the free community and not remain in a back ward for decades or, perhaps, for their whole life in a major psychiatric center.

"It is further questionable that authors use the general term 'mentally ill' as if to suggest that the 500,000 men and women, serving time in jails and prisons, are all troubled by some severe psychiatric disorder, such as schizophrenia or some other psychosis. In fact, the great majority of so-called mentally ill patients, are probably individuals being treated for common life problems, such as depression, anxiety, adjustment disorders, and some of whom might receive some measure of psychiatric medication, which actually stabilizes them, reasonably effectively in most cases."

Dr. Barilla continued, speaking from his own experience: "It is also my opinion here that any kind of treatment for inmate-patients or criminals without any significant mental or emotional problems, if effective, means moving the convicted felons in a more pro-social, law-abiding, autonomous direction with their lives in order to help them become productive, competent members of society. It seems to be a common American phenomenon to blame the system, program, or some authority, when an individual exhibits incompetent, criminal, or self-defeating behaviors, and not to place the primary burden of responsibility on the individuals themselves. Rehabilitation interventions in prisons will inevitably fail if assumptions are made that inmates can simply be passive recipients in good programs and that lasting, positive change will occur without inmates' authentic motivation and perseverance in the rehabilitation process. Let us not forget the extreme importance of effective use of behavior-management principles in any efforts at rehabilitation.

"It would seem then, that the mission is possible, challenging, and rewarding, despite limitations of success in the matter of inmate rehabilitation and despite the daunting data of the high recidivism rates among released prisoners."

*****

In Doc B.'s doctoral dissertation on predicting prisoner misconduct, one important finding was that younger inmates doing smaller sentences were the most troublesome, undisciplined, and penalized individuals in maximum-security prison. Captain Rauch often teased Doctor Barilla, saying, "Shit, Doc, I could have told you that without doing all that fancy research."

Doc B. said to the group, "As we remember the earlier story of Eddie Hermann's murder of several family members, it is interesting to note later findings in a book entitled, *Kids Who Kill*. The author, law professor and forensic psychologist, Charles P. Ewing, found a 'new breed of killers.' He wrote that over 10 percent of murders in America are committed by youth"

Doc B. felt compelled to share his fantasy that perhaps some wayward incarcerated youth might be inspired by the repentant, rehabilitated Prince Henry, from Shakespeare's *King Henry IV*, who said:

Like bright metal on a sullen ground,

My reformation, glittering over my faults,

Shall show more goodly and attract more eyes,

Than that which has no foil to set it off!

Doc then added: "The formerly antisocial, wayward prince ultimately transformed himself into a man of honor, was cour geous in battle, and went on to become King Henry V."

Then, Doc exclaimed, "Now there's a great role model for determination and positive change!"

GLOSSARY OF TERMS

Ain't but a minute—This expression is used when an inmate asks a newcomer how long his sentence is. If it's a short sentence, he might say, "Ain't gonna be here but a minute."

Baby-Fucker—Child molester

Beef—This translates to the crime an inmate committed (e.g., "Hey Joe, you got a five to ten. What's your beef?—Response, "I committed a robbery.").

Bid or a bit—This term represents the sentence an inmate is doing (e.g., "Hey Joe, what's your bid?"—Response, "Five years.").

Bogue—This means that something is really foul, unpleasant, or undesirable. It is believed to come from the word bogus.

Bullet—Usually a county-jail sentence, anything less than 365 days (a year minus one day).

Cashes in a ticket—This is when an inmate, who has been offended, challenges the threatening inmate.

Cell gangster—That is an inmate who acts like a tough guy, very boastful and threatening to other inmates, while he is locked down in his cell but becomes meek and mild when he comes out of his cell and is face to face with the other inmates. An expression used to describe an inmate who likes to act like a gangster is, "He wants to be a James Cagney," meaning he wants to be like the tough-talking actor in the popular gangster movies that came out in the 1930s and 1940s.

Don't let your mouth override your ass—Don't make threats unless you have the ass (muscle) to back it up.

Down the dirt highway or **Down the Hershey highway** or **Packing Fudge**—Anal sex among inmates so inclined.

Dressed fly—This is a popular street term that means that an inmate is very sharp. He dresses in very sharp clothes that make him look very appealing, especially to the opposite sex.

Dropped a dime—This means that an inmate has snitched on someone or ratted them out. The inmate has become a stool pigeon, the worst offense any inmate can commit. It is telling something about someone that will put them in a bad light. If an inmate is really trying to hurt somebody, they say he "dropped a half dollar." That is as bad as it can get. The only ones who usually do this are the ones that are trying to gain favor with the correctional personnel and usually end up, for their safety, in protective custody for the rest of the time they are imprisoned or they may be transferred out to another prison where they are unknown.

Faggot—A frequently used expression to describe inmates who offer oral or anal sex to others. *Important*: most inmates who put their penis into others' orifices don't consider themselves homosexual. They say that only the recipient of their penis is a faggot.

Frontin'—When an inmate poses as something he really is not, and he acts like a big shot. He builds himself up beyond reality or possibility.

Gettin' down with the git down—This is when someone is really getting into something, doing something very enjoyable. For example, dancing or partying with a favorite woman.

Gettin' what your hand calls for—The usually negative observation that someone deserves bad shit to happen to them for violating some code of behavior, even a perverted code (e.g., a stool pigeon gets stabbed and beaten for reporting criminal activities to authorities).

GOOD JAIL!, GOOD JAIL!—A popular mantra to reassure anyone in prison that it's an alright place to be.

Good lookin' out—Means that another inmate has done something favorable, something positive, for a buddy or homeboy.

Hack—What inmates call a corrections officer.

Hack's mate—What inmates critically call a person who collaborates with corrections officers.

Homeboy or **Homie**—Originally, this meant somebody who came from the same hometown as the inmate. Now the meaning includes a good friend who is treated like a lifelong buddy.

I caught a wire—This is the phrase used when an inmate hears news about something important or just news in general. It refers to the pipeline in a prison where inmates know more than the COs or administration believe the inmates know.

I copped to the behavior—This is when an inmate might admit to an infraction or, in court, agree for a bargain and admit what he did was wrong.

I fell on a beef—This is the term used when an inmate talks about getting busted for some crime. For example, he was arrested for committing a robbery or a rape.

I got paper—This is when an inmate goes out on parole or an inmate, when facing charges in court, gets probation instead of being sentenced to jail. This is called paper. In other words, he does not have to do much jail time or any jail time; he just got paper and has to report to a probation officer for a specified amount of time following his release.

I got your back—This translates as an inmate watching out for and even trying to protect another inmate.

I'm down with that—This means that two or more inmates agree on something. They will go along with the program.

I'm short—This is when an inmate is very close to going out on parole or very close to the end of his sentence. For example, if an inmate has only forty-four days left of his sentence, he might say, "I've got forty-three days and a wake-up." He is saying that last day is when he wakes up to go out the front gate of the prison.

Inmate-Patients—The name used to describe prison inmates who receive mental-health care in lock-up situations. It's important that the hyphenated description begins with the word "inmate" because it must be remembered that, first and foremost, the individual is a convicted felon requiring a high level of security and supervision.

Juhggin—This is an inmate term that is used when an inmate is messing with another inmate, especially when one is trying to agitate another person.

Made my bones—When one fulfills initiation requirements to gain acceptance or membership to some group or organization.

Misguided benevolence scale—An imaginary continuum of people, especially prison personnel, being slightly naïve about prisoner realities at one end, to those at the other end of the scale being totally unenlightened, to the point that they put all staff in grave danger with their actions.

Miss Ann—The expression is used primarily by blacks to indicate when a white woman is in the presence of a black man and seems to connote an amorous or romantic situation. It may have originated with Little Orphan Annie, who had those big eyes with no pupils as though she does not see color. Color blind = no prejudice.

Mutha-fucka—The most common hyphenated expression used in prison, mostly by inmates, sometimes by staff, to describe virtually anything or anybody. It can be used as a noun or an adjective.

Mutt—This is someone who is loathed—someone who is not worth anyone's time. It is very uncomplimentary and derogatory. Corrections officers will use the term for inmates who exhibit despicable behavior or have committed despicable crimes.

My kid, my bitch—Means an inmate has claimed another inmate as a homosexual toy, to be used whenever they want. Not exactly a slave but close.

Off the count—Translates as an inmate being dead, murdered, or escaped. When an inmate intends to kill someone, they say they are going to take him off the count, or "I'm gonna off him."

On the down low—This is an expression used in speaking about men who are homosexual. It is something that is to be kept very quiet or secret because it is a dishonor to masculinity and the machismo image (*See* faggot).

On the real side—This translates as the way things actually, truly, realistically are. This is not some political BS or not some fantasy but actually the real deal.

Oreo, also known as **Oreo Cookie** or **Uncle Tom**—This is the term used by black inmates for other black inmates who suck up to "whitey" or the "Honky" authority and betray their black race by doing that. The Oreo means they are black on the outside but are really white on the inside.

Outcount—When an inmate is temporarily housed in one prison, usually to receive special services, but that inmate belongs on the permanent count of the sending prison. Typically, the inmate will be returned to the sending prison after a short period of time.

Peep your hole card—The person who says this means: I know what you're all about; I know your next move; I know what you're hiding from me; etc.

Riding his wood—Any male masturbating.

Round (on somebody)—This means an inmate is being evasive or not making a commitment, and it usually is pretty obvious.

Running concurrently—This indicates that an inmate who has been charged with, for example, three counts of robbery, each one carrying a five to ten year sentence, has gotten a break from the court because the court has decided to allow the terms to run concurrently (e.g., the inmate will serve only one five to ten year sentence instead of a fifteen-year minimum sentence). These deals are usually the result of plea bargaining with the prosecution.

Running wild—This indicates an inmate is serving consecutive terms. For example, an inmate is charged with three robberies each carrying a five to ten year sentence. The total sentence would amount to serving a minimum of fifteen years and a maximum of thirty years in prison.

Sells a ticket—This is when an inmate challenges another inmate in some way, insulting him or saying something that is offensive to the other inmate.

Skatin'—When someone is floating around the prison, not being where they are supposed to be.

Skid bid—A short sentence in prison.

Spot—An area in the yard where inmates exercise and where individual groups have claimed their workout spots. One does not go on another's spot without the expressed verbal permission of the leader of that group. Doing so would lead to dire consequences.

Step off—Literally means any one of the following: I don't want to hear that. Get outta my face. Move away. Move down the road here a little bit.

Strapped down—Carrying a concealed weapon (a homemade shank).

Superintendent—Warden of a prison; the two words are used interchangeably.

The Dozens—This is a game played in prison and on the street in which the mother of an inmate, for example, is put in a despicable situation by another inmate (e.g. "Your mother walks the street with a mattress on her back."). The second inmate retaliates by returning the jab with a more despicable situation (e.g. "Your mother blows dead Japs."). Playing this game can be very dangerous because inmates can be very callous in their name-calling and this can end up in a physical confrontation.

There's a new Jack on the job—This means that a new employee, usually a corrections officer, in a cellblock.

Throw down—This is when an inmate prepares to fight somebody. He states that he is going to throw down on a certain person.

To break-off—Another expression for when one inmate attacks another inmate or any other person.

Validated—When it has been determined that an inmate has significant gang membership he is known to have been validated as a gang member.

Wolf ticket—This is when an inmate creates a serious potential for violence; a serious threat or insult.

You got a good hand—This translates as something similar to having been dealt a good set of cards in a poker game. In other words, for an inmate to be told that, means that his life in the penitentiary is pretty good.

Zip bid—In this case it means that an inmate is doing time from between zero and a certain number of years (e.g. 0-5, 0-7, 0-15) and they have a chance for an early release and parole. An interesting piece of information here is that if the parole board is not in favor of releasing an inmate who has earned an opportunity to be paroled, the most that the board can do to that inmate is keep him in prison for another two years. Then, automatically, so long as the prisoner continues with good behavior, he must again come before the board and hope for release. However, the board can again hold the inmate over for another two years. If the inmate is in for a life sentence, this process of holding him every two years can go on indefinitely.

ABOUT THE AUTHOR

Michael Boccia, Ph.D., has been a psychologist and business consultant for forty-one years and has served in numerous clinical and organizational settings during that time. His theoretical orientation has been cognitive-behavioral and his philosophical perspective is to generally maximize autonomy in clients. In the workplace, the goals are optimal enhancement of job performance and job satisfaction at all levels in organizations.

Dr. Boccia is currently focusing his professional work almost exclusively in mental-health consultation with active-duty military populations on military bases. He has worked in private practice, with corrections and law enforcement, corporate populations, leadership coaching, and doing a wide variety of workshops and training. One special interest has been Emotional Intelligence, which offers a unique method of mind/emotion management and significantly strengthens leadership potential in any organization.

Dr. Boccia studied a variety of disciplines in his undergraduate work including history, philosophy, and engineering while ultimately earning a Ph.D. in psychology. More recently, he earned the status of Certified Correctional Health Professional (CCHP). He is a member of many professional and civic organizations and frequently teaches as an adjunct at local colleges. Dr. Boccia resides in southwest Florida but his professional activities will not be exclusively confined to any particular geographic region.

About the Co-Author

Peter Mars is a forty-year veteran of law enforcement, twenty-five of those years concurrent as a Christian minister serving several denominations during that time and more recently as an adjunct college professor in Maine, teaching criminal justice.

Mars is the author of five true-crime books: *The Tunnel, A Taste for Money, The Key, The Chaplain,* and *Alternative Measures,* and the coauthor with John Butler (retired chief of police for Mansfield, Ohio, and Sanibel Island, Florida) of *The Best Suit in Town.* He is also the writer of three books for other authors. His latest work, *The Gold of Troy,* will be due out late 2011. He recently assisted Dr. Menelaos Mickey Demos in putting together a book called *Life in Mani—Today,* a story about the freedom of living in southern Greece.

Mars currently lives with his wife, Margery, in south-central Maine.